WASHOE COUNTY LIBRARY

3 1235 03077 1302

P9-CJE-378

Introducing
Vivien Leigh Reid

Introducing
Vivien Leigh Reid

Daughter of the Diva

Yvonne Collins and Sandy Rideout

St. Martin's Griffin ✥ New York

INTRODUCING VIVIEN LEIGH REID: DAUGHTER OF THE DIVA. Copyright © 2005 by Yvonne Collins and Sandy Rideout. All rights reserved. Printed in the United States of America. No part of this book may be used or reproduced in any manner whatsoever without written permission except in the case of brief quotations embodied in critical articles or reviews. For information, address St. Martin's Press, 175 Fifth Avenue, New York, NY 10010.

www.stmartins.com

Book design by Irene Vallye

Library of Congress Cataloging-in-Publication Data

Collins, Yvonne.
    Introducing Vivien Leigh Reid : daughter of the diva / Yvonne Collins and Sandy Rideout.—1st ed.
        p. cm.
    Summary: A fifteen-year-old is less than thrilled to be reunited for a summer in Ireland with the mother who left for fame and fortune in Los Angeles when she was three.
    ISBN 0-312-33837-6
    EAN 978-0312-33837-4
    [1. Actors and actresses—Fiction. 2. Mothers and daughters—Fiction. 3. Ireland—Fiction.] I. Rideout, Sandy. II. Title.

PZ7.C6839In 2005
[Fic]—dc22

                                                                    2004060160

First Edition: May 2005

10 9 8 7 6 5 4 3 2 1

acknowledgments

We have been fortunate to have met divas of all ages and to have studied them in their natural habitats. As much as we like to give credit for inspiration where it is due, this is one situation where it's probably better not to name any names!

In the diva-free zone, we must thank our agent, Jenny Bent, for seeing this book's potential and for getting it into the right hands. Thanks also to our editor, Elizabeth Bewley, who took a shine to Leigh and made sure she got first-class treatment all the way.

As always, we are grateful to our family and friends for their continued interest and support—and for trying to keep all the details straight.

Last, and most important, special thanks to Dave for his patience, cheerleading, and head for business.

Introducing
Vivien Leigh Reid

one

If he drools, I will scream. I will scream so loud that the doors will blow right off this plane. I will scream so loud that eardrums will burst on five continents. I will scream so loud that The Man Formerly Known as My Father will hear me halfway around the world.

I can't believe the flight attendant has disappeared. It's so typical. At first, I couldn't get rid of her, because Dad asked her to keep an eye on me. But now that I could actually use some help, she's off serving drinks in business class, leaving me at the mercy of the creepy old guy in the next seat.

There I was, minding my own business and watching *Chicago,* the in-flight movie, when *thunk:* the Geezer's cranium hits my shoulder right in the middle of the "Cell Block Tango." Out of the corner of my eye, I can see his pink scalp gleaming through the gray hair he's raked over a bald spot. And his whistle-breathing is going to turn into a snore any minute, I just know it. It's a total nightmare. What if his head rolls forward? I swear, if he gets anywhere near my chest, I will scream so loud his comb-over will land in Istanbul. Wherever that is.

This is what comes of being too nice. We were barely off the ground when the Geez loosened his tie and turned to stare at the side of my head. I sensed a lame attempt to "connect with the teenager" coming on and should have bolted for the washroom while I had the chance. Unfortunately, I was raised to be polite.

"I'll bet you're a big Justin Timberland fan," he said, directing a blast of garlic breath my way.

It might have killed a weaker girl, but luckily I have a healthy body mass index. Or so my gym teacher tells me. It's her subtle way of letting me know that my athletic build is perfectly normal. I think it would be more normal if I were actually an athlete, but whatever.

"Timber*lake*," I corrected the Geez.

"Right," he said. "I'm thinking of the boot, not the boy. Well, anyway, I hear he's *da business.*"

Personally, I think paying full fare for a seat—as my Former Father did—should entitle a passenger to read her novel in peace. But did I say so? No, I did not. I took the high road. "I'm into gangsta rap," I said.

Anyone else would have taken one look at my khaki capris and pink hoodie and laughed out loud, but he didn't even respond. That's because he had dozed off, *right in the middle of my sentence.* His head was actually bobbing over his chest. Now, I don't kid myself that I am the most fascinating girl on the planet, but this was completely insulting. I was thinking about giving him a little jab with my pencil, when he suddenly snapped upright on his own.

"I've heard all about that Ten Cents," he said.

As if there'd been no lag time in the conversation at all! Unbelievable. "Yeah, 50 Cent is the bomb all right," I said, holding my book so close to my face that my Stila lip gloss stuck the pages together.

"I never let my daughter fly alone when she was your age."

No kidding. That's because he knows guys like him would have her grabbing a parachute.

"I'm an orphan."

Which is almost true, because I'm planning on firing Dad.

★ ★ ★

I used to like my father. In fact, he had earned a consistent four-star rating until he decided to enroll me, against my will, in the J. D. Sandford Academy, a "learning lab" that's supposed to foster creative thinking but is really just a holding cell for supergeeks. Now that he's shipped me off to a foreign country for the summer, his ratings have dropped right off the charts.

Had I any desire to travel, it wouldn't be to Ireland, where, as far as I can tell from my Internet searches, it never stops raining. Ireland happens to be where my mother is working, however, and my father, for reasons related to his premature senility, has decided it's time the two of us bonded. As if. I haven't seen the woman in nearly two years, but there is no gaping hole in my life. Dad and I manage just fine.

Or so I thought, until I overheard him on the phone with her.

"You need to take Leigh this summer," he said, as I watched from my bedroom door. "She's been moody and miserable for months. No, it's worse than that: she's been downright bitchy." He ran a hand through his hair until it stood on end. "Her grades have dropped and I'm at my wit's end."

Bitchy? That was a little harsh. Moody, maybe. But he's hardly Mr. Congeniality himself these days. Consider the tantrum he threw when I spilled my trademark Hard Candy Trance purple nail polish on the passenger seat of his new sports car. The way he carried on, you'd think I'd done it on purpose. Like I'd waste my favorite nail polish simply to annoy him.

He totally overreacts to everything. I experimented with a vegetarian diet for a couple of weeks and he freaked out because he thought I was going anorexic on him. When I tried to educate him, he refused to think about the issue from a cow's perspective. There is no room for informed debate in our house. I had to promise to eat meat three times a week just to keep him off my case. One day, when I'm allowed an opinion of my own, I'm becoming a vegan.

"This isn't normal for girls her age, Ann," he continued. "This is serious. The Academy will put her on probation if she doesn't keep her honors standing. She's had a tough year and she needs a female role model. I haven't asked much of you, but it's time you did your share." My mother obviously protested, because Dad's face got redder and redder as he listened. "Look, she's extremely independent for a fourteen-year-old and she reads all the time. When you're shooting, she can stay in your trailer, and between scenes, you can get to know your own daughter."

That's when I first realized he was losing it: I turned fifteen *months* ago! And who could blame me for a few mood swings after the year I've had? It hasn't just been tough, it's been *brutal*. First, Glen Myers dumped me at the Halloween dance in front of the entire school population. Then, Abby MacKenzie, my best friend in the world, packed up and moved to New York with her family at Christmas leaving me on the periphery of the J. D. Sandford social scene for the rest of the school year.

"You have plenty of other friends," Dad said.

"I don't have a *best* friend." I gave him the "you can't possibly understand" look. It's not like you can—or should—replace a best friend overnight.

"Promote someone off the B-team."

"I'm auditioning," I told him. "It takes time. Besides, it's not like Abby is dead, you know."

But sometimes it feels as if she might as well be, even though we text message each other ten times a day:

```
Abs,
pls teL me
yor dad h8z
Hs nu job.
L
```

```
L
gud nuz, he told my
mom Hs nu boss
iz an idiot. mAbE
he'll quit s%n.
A


Abs,
gr8! U c%d b
bak b4 skul stRtz. ☺
L


L
cancel wot I sed b4.
Dad jst caLd. Hs
boss got fired 2day and
Dad got Hs job. ☹
A


Abs,
weL, dun wori,
ther's stil d hex.
L
```

Before they left Seattle, Abby and I got a book from the library called *Bewitched: Simple Spells for Everyday Life* and put three separate hexes on her father using hair and fingernail clippings that Abby had collected in a baggie. Now I am wondering if the hair belonged to Mrs. MacKenzie; she's had a suspicious streak of bad luck in New York, including a freak attack by a pigeon in Central Park that required a couple of stitches. Just in case, we've decided to reverse the spells next time Abby visits.

Anyway, my point is, my father should understand that best friends separated at this crucial time of life have to go through a grieving process. And grieving people can be moody. He'd know this if he read the copy of *On Death and Dying* that Grandma gave him when Grampa got sick three years ago. The book says there are five stages everyone goes through: Denial, Anger, Bargaining, Depression, and finally, Acceptance. Grandma got through all five in record time and hooked up with Stan-Stan-the-Garbageman (or "Waste Management Engineer," as she says) in less than a year.

I guess I've mostly been stuck in the "anger" phase since Abby left, although some days I achieve mere "depression." What I really needed was a relaxing summer, where I could focus on devising *Survivor*-style tests for the rest of my friends, to see who might at some point be worthy of promotion into the "best friend" category. By fall, I would have had it all worked out. Now my schedule is blown. Ireland—and my mother—can only make things worse.

I barely had time to get Grandma, who hates my mother, on my side before Dad sat me down, the e-mail confirmation of my flight in his hand. The discussion—and I use the term loosely—involved a lot of crying (mine), a lot of reasoning (Grandma's), and a lot of yelling (Dad's).

He seems to be under the impression that he's the boss of me until I turn eighteen.

The man is practically begging to be fired.

★   ★   ★

I prepared for the worst, but it never occurred to me that the trip would include some old geezer practically drooling on my shoulder. Or that I'd have to rely on a lady wearing a nerdy suit and a big smile for rescue. This is outrageous.

Fortunately, I have already planned my revenge. Being an amateur in the parenting arena, my mother will be easily fooled. I'll collect the guilt money she always forks over and hit the coolest stores in Dublin to buy clothes. Then, when she's at work one day, I'll head to the roughest part of town and get a huge tattoo on my chest or shoulder—something along the lines of a wolverine. After that, I'll get half a dozen piercings in visible places, maybe even one in my tongue. Dad's fed me a line about the risk of brain infection from tongue piercing, but I know he's just trying to protect his investment in straightening my teeth.

My goal is to make him faint when I step off the plane in six weeks. If I go home at all, that is. I could just send him a postcard of a sheep, on the back of which I've written *"YOU'RE FIRED."* No signature. Then I'll lie about my age, get myself a job in a pub, and finish school by correspondence.

For the moment, however, I am pinned in my seat by the Geezer, who is snuggling into my shoulder. It took me an hour to coax some body into my limp locks this morning and now it's being squashed flat. Worse, the scent of my special-occasion-only Cinnamon Buns shampoo is being overpowered by the stench of garlic because the guy is starting to snore in loud, snuffling gusts. People in the middle row are turning to stare. One lady actually elbows her husband and they chuckle together over my plight. Obviously I am the only one left in the world who troubles herself to be nice.

At last, Martina, the flight attendant, trundles down the aisle pulling her beverage cart. I stare at the back of her head, willing her to turn around. When she does, her eyebrows shoot up in surprise and in spite of myself, my eyes water up.

Holding a finger to her lips, she tiptoes over and with one smooth motion, takes Geezer Guy by the shoulder and hoists him upright. A startled snort erupts as his eyes pop open. "Where am I?" he asks, blinking at her.

"Halfway to Ireland, sir," Martina says. "Let me get you a complimentary drink." She turns to me, smiling, as she pours his bourbon. "There are some seats free a few rows ahead, Leigh. You'd be able to see the movie better from there, so why don't you grab your things and move?"

The auditions are over: Martina is my new best friend.

After *Chicago* ends, I walk back down the aisle and offer my blanket to the old guy. He's not so bad, I guess, and it's not his fault that my life sucks.

two

Grandma always whispers the word "actress" as if it's a crime. As far as I can tell, the only crime my mother is committing is that she's a lousy actress. Not that I am the best person to make a fair assessment: she left my father and me when I was only three to find fame and fortune in Los Angeles. Although she visited often in the first couple of years, the visits eventually got further and further apart; she never once asked me to visit her in L.A. I see her if she happens to film in Seattle or Vancouver, but otherwise, it's down to a few phone calls a year. I wish she wouldn't bother, but what am I supposed to say? There's no nice, polite way to tell your mother not to call. Dad won't do it either, because he's afraid I'll regret it later.

"You never know, Leigh," he said. "One day she might grow up and you'll be glad to know her." This was unusually critical of him, because he has a rule against dissing her in front of me.

Every so often, Mom ships me a package containing her latest script. *"Vivien,"* she scrawls on the cover in big loopy handwriting. *"Here's something for your collection. It was the role of a lifetime! Enjoy, darling. Love, Annika Anderson."*

No one but my mother calls me by my first name, but Vivien Leigh is Mom's idol. She played a young southern belle named Scarlett O'Hara in a "classic" movie called *Gone with the Wind.*

Mom's praying for a remake, although Grandma—who isn't confined by a no-dissing rule—says Mom is getting a little "long in the tooth" to play Scarlett.

I try to read the scripts she sends but some are so pathetic I can't get past the first page. Mom's specialty is low-budget, made-for-TV vixens and tramps. For example, she's a regular as the "other woman" on the Sunday night *Passionate Hearts* series. Recently, she played a demon that lures a priest from the arms of God. *"The highlight of my career to date,"* she wrote on the script. It's pretty sad.

Since Dad broke the news to me about my summer plans, I've imagined how my first conversation with my mother will go a hundred times.

Scene 2: Leigh Strikes a Deal

A tall, sophisticated teenager steps off the plane, turning heads as she goes. No one knows that her athletic build is being enhanced by a new padded bra, which she wrestled into in the plane's tiny washroom to avoid causing her Former Father's premature death. As she glides past the airport's windows, the sophisticated teen's light-brown hair gleams in the sunlight. She approaches a stylish blonde in a black Armani pantsuit and graciously extends her hand.

LEIGH

Hello, Mother.

ANNIKA

Leigh, how nice to see you. You look *gorgeous* and you've developed such a sense of style!

LEIGH

Thank you, you look well yourself.
But let's cut to the chase, Mother: I
don't want to be here any more than you
want me here, so what are we going to do
about it?

ANNIKA

But I *do* want you here, Leigh! I'm thrilled
that we finally have the chance to get to
know each other.

LEIGH

Now, we both know we're only in this bind
because of Dad. To be honest, I think he's
going senile. Anyway, I've worked out a
plan: I'll make the odd appearance on
your set where I'll be nice and polite.
You'll look like the perfect mother. In
return, you'll leave me alone to enjoy
myself. As Dad told you, I'm very independent.

*The blond woman is momentarily distracted by two very
cute Irishmen who are hovering nearby.*

LEIGH

Mother?

ANNIKA

Excuse me, darling. They must want my
autograph.

LEIGH
Actually, they're waiting for me. They've
offered to show me around the city.

ANNIKA
[trying to disguise her embarrassment]
Oh, of course. Well, it's obvious that you're
exceptionally mature, so I'll respect your
wishes. I'll make sure you have enough
money and someone to drive you around.
Otherwise, you're on your own. Let me know
if you need anything.

LEIGH
I appreciate how understanding you're
being.

ANNIKA
I'm just sorry it's only six weeks.

*The blond woman reaches into her purse and pulls out a
thick stack of euro cash and a credit card. She hands
them to the sophisticated teenager. The two shake hands
again, climb into separate limos and drive off toward
Dublin, where nonstop adventure awaits.*

Okay, so it's not Shakespeare, but the scripts she sends aren't exactly Oscar material either. The point is, I'm determined to keep my
cool and make this work, no matter how annoying she is. And unless she's changed recently, my mother is a very annoying woman.

One really annoying thing about her is that she is beautiful. I
spot her golden hair the moment I disembark, cascading in ringlets
down her back. Instead of the Armani pantsuit, however, she's

wearing a very short suede skirt, a tight pink sweater, and stiletto boots. She obviously hasn't read my script. If I weren't so polite, I'd tell her that she needs a new stylist.

Even from a distance, I notice there's something different about her. She's even thinner, if that's possible, but as she gets closer, I see that her lips are three times the size they were in that demon-temptress role. I read the magazines, I watch *Entertainment Tonight:* Mom has discovered collagen.

I can tell from her expression that she doesn't recognize me. When I raise my eyebrows quizzically, her hand goes to her mouth, her eyes wide with . . . what, *horror?* It can't be my clothes. I've abandoned the baggy, grunge-rock phase that nearly caused her emotional collapse the last time she visited Seattle. Now, I prefer clothes that fit and I'm into a more casual look—kind of J. Crew, but hipper. Maybe she's surprised that I'm even taller than she is now. Or maybe that Geezer really did a number on my hair.

Recovering quickly—she is a pro, after all—Mom stretches her swollen lips into a smile and hurries toward me. She's clutching a shopping bag, out of which protrudes the blond head of a doll in a black, fur-trimmed coat. Not a Madame Alexander doll! I already have a dozen at home taking up valuable closet space.

"Another doll?" I ask, flinching as she wraps one arm around my shoulder in a half-hug. "I'm fifteen, in case you've forgotten."

"Darling, a girl is never too old for dolls, especially collector's items like this one." She pulls it out of the bag. "Allow me to intro-duce the Grand Hotel Greta Garbo! I thought she might remind you of me."

I don't need a doll for that. All I need to do is look at the mole on my left cheek and I think of her because she has the exact same one on hers. She calls it a "beauty mark" and seems to like it, whereas I think it's hideous and plan to have it removed the first chance I get. Dad won't hear of it, big surprise. I practically had to go on a hunger strike before he'd let me get my ears pierced.

It figures that the only thing I'd inherit from Mom is her least attractive feature. I wouldn't complain if I'd gotten the blue eyes or blond curls. Instead, I have Dad's mousy hair and muddy green eyes that are the exact color of guacamole that's been left out too long. Worse, I also have his gargantuan feet.

At least I didn't inherit Mom's breathy voice or the way she enunciates every syllable, as if her vocal coach is grading her. I notice she's also acquired some sort of weird accent since I last saw her. Not Irish, exactly, but a mish-mash she picked up over the Atlantic. It makes her sound pretentious.

She tries to press Greta into my arms and I back away quickly. "I am *not* holding that thing," I hiss, ditching my script. "I can't believe you didn't recognize me."

"Vivien, darling, I was just shocked by how you've changed. You've become a woman since I saw you last." Obviously, the bra is making an impression. She lowers her voice and adds, "I suppose there are a few things we should talk about, woman to woman."

Oh my god. She wants to have *The Talk*. There's got to be a rule about the number of parenting hours people need to serve before they earn the right to torture their kids in this way.

"Dad told me everything there is to know years ago, *when I needed it.*"

"Vivien! Are you suggesting that I don't spend enough time with you?"

Why state the obvious? Besides, there's no point in annoying her when I'm planning to spend six weeks on the town accompanied only by her cash and credit cards. "I'm not suggesting anything. And it's *Leigh.*"

"Now, I named you Vivien after a very talented lady. You should be proud."

"Well, it's better than Scarlett, I guess, so thanks, Annika."

"Please call me Mother."

"But you sign your scripts 'Annika Anderson.' I just thought . . ."

"I sign those in my capacity as an *actress*. They'll be worth something someday." I'll get right on eBay when we get to the swanky hotel. "Now hurry up, darling, my driver is waiting to take us to Bray."

"I thought we were staying in Dublin."

"We're staying in County Wicklow, just outside of Dublin. That's where we're filming. Bray is the quaintest little fishing village."

"*A fishing village?*" My stomach sinks. Tattoo parlors will likely be hard to find.

"I've got the sweetest cottage by the sea. I thought it would help me find my inner Irishwoman. For my role, you know." Since my mother comes from a long line of Swedes, she'll likely be looking awhile. "Just wait till you see our room," she adds.

So much for my dream of the swanky hotel. It's so unfair. She always stays in swanky hotels. Why did she have to pick this trip to mix with the locals? And what's this about *our room?* "You mean I don't get my own room?"

"I didn't know you'd be visiting until a few weeks ago, did I, darling? But don't worry, it's a lovely, big room and you'll have your own cot. We'll hardly be there anyway because we'll be on set most of the time." She titters self-consciously and glances over her shoulder, where two scruffy men are watching her, entranced. She smiles flirtatiously at them before whispering, "I think they recognize me."

"I'm surprised the lips haven't thrown them off." Oops. Did I just use my out-loud voice?

She steps back abruptly and stares at me. "What do you mean?"

It's too late to back off now. "Your doctor went a little overboard, Mom, they're *huge.*"

She looks wounded. "Are you trying to hurt my feelings?" Duh! Of course I'm trying to hurt her feelings! "Because you have no idea what it's like to be a woman my age in the film business, Vivien."

Her huge blue eyes are glassy, as if she's working up to a cry. I suspect it's just drama, but I relent and say, "You're only forty-one, hardly over the hill yet."

"Sssshhh," she hisses. "Don't even say that number out loud! That's eighty-two in Hollywood years." But she looks mollified as she hooks her arm chummily through mine and starts pulling me toward the door. "We're going to have a *wonderful* time."

"Right." I suppose separate limos are out of the question.

"Try to be more positive, darling." One of the scruffy men springs forward and seizes my carry-on bag as an excuse to speak to Mom. She gives him a dazzling smile and tosses her ringlets. "Thank you so much! I'm Annika Anderson and this is . . . *Vivien.*"

Annika Anderson, siren of the silver screen, apparently doesn't have a teenage daughter: she has a "Vivien."

```
A
Arrived safely n Ireland.
I'm homesick alredi.
Mom worse thN eva.
stNd by 4 stories
L
```

three

Mrs. O'Reilly is already standing at the kitchen stove frying bacon in a cast-iron pan when I get up the next morning. She owns the cottage the movie production is renting for my mother and takes care of the cooking and cleaning. Yanking her bathrobe closed over a ratty pink nightgown, Mrs. O'Reilly mumbles something completely unintelligible to me around the cigarette stuck to her lower lip. Although I expected an accent, it's like she's speaking a completely different language.

"Pardon me?" I ask, careful to sound like the well-bred American I am.

Shuffling a few steps closer in unlaced work boots, she repeats her comment, the hand-rolled cigarette bobbing up and down with each word: "*Cead mile failte,* I said. A hundred thousand welcomes. It's a Gaelic expression." Thick, wiry eyebrows joining over her nose in a permanent scowl make her look anything but welcoming.

"Thanks." I try not to stare as she turns back to the stove. No wonder the sheep were making such a racket outside my bedroom window this morning. If she walked down the lane from the main house in that get-up it must have given them quite a fright.

"Well, yer as pretty as yer ma, that's for sure," she says, turning back to me.

Please. I'll buy that I'm prettier than my father, but I certainly can't compete with my mother. Mrs. O'Reilly is trying to get on my good side for some reason but I won't be falling for it. Sitting down at the kitchen table, I ask, "Is it always this cold in June?" I am shivering in an Old Navy camisole and shorts.

"Go on outta that, it's a grand morning." She leans over and pinches my upper arm hard enough to leave a bruise. "Yer a desperate frail gersha, you are." Frail? Obviously, the woman has failed to notice my healthy BMI. "Put on some more duds and take a dander after breakfast. You could use some fresh air."

I'm guessing she's suggesting a walk. Like that's going to happen. We're in the middle of nowhere, where would I go?

As if reading my mind, she says, "If you want to see *Glen*maline or *Glen*cree, turn right at the end of the lane. If it's *Glen*macnass yer after, you'll be wanting to head in the other direction."

It figures. Every landform in this godforsaken country is known by the name of my ex-boyfriend. Hearing "Glen" constantly isn't going to help me get over him.

"What a lovely morning," my mother chirps from the kitchen door. Her stupid fake accent adds to my depression. Why couldn't I have a normal mother? Abby's mother doesn't suddenly have a New York accent. Of course, Mrs. MacKenzie is an actuary rather than an actress—a normal profession.

Sliding a plate in front of me, Mrs. O'Reilly whispers to my mother, "She's got the hump today."

"Still sulking?" Mom asks, making no pretense at whispering. "Her father warned me about that. First broken heart, you know."

Dad swore he wouldn't tell her. I am going to kill him right after I fire him. Mom couldn't possibly understand what I am going through. I'll bet she's never been dumped in her life because she's gorgeous, even first thing in the morning. Mind you, the bright red lipstick—the Annika Anderson trademark—is a little jarring in this country kitchen.

While she and Mrs. O'Reilly discuss my mental health, I consider the feast before me: fried eggs, fried bacon, fried bread, fried tomato, and a mysterious black blob glistening with grease.

"Blood pudding," my mother offers helpfully, when she sees me poking at it with my fork.

"Not from *real blood*," I say.

"Yes, real blood—but not from humans." As if that's supposed to make me feel better. She smiles as she takes the seat across from me. "Don't think about it too much. Just try it, it's delicious."

"You first." She's so pale without her stage makeup that she could use the extra blood.

"Oh, I couldn't," she says, sipping her tea. "My figure, you know." Big bones are another thing I inherited from Dad. I am not fat, but I feel like a giant compared to my mother. At five foot eight inches she is barely a size four and she looks frail enough to be knocked over by the draft that is blowing through the kitchen. And yet, the single slice of dry toast on the plate in front of her proves that Mrs. O'Reilly has already been informed about the pressures of Hollywood. "But *you* should try it," she adds encouragingly. "A fry-up is part of the Irish experience."

Hovering over me with a teapot in her hand, Mrs. O'Reilly says, "Yer jammy to be given such lashings when so many starved during the great praitie famine. Cuppa cha?" I stare at her blankly. "Can you not understand English?" she says, exasperated. "Jaysus, where are me fags when I need 'em?"

My mother reaches for a tin box and hands it to her. Setting the teapot on the table, Mrs. O'Reilly lights another hand-rolled cigarette, although the previous one is still attached to her lip.

"What Mrs. O'Reilly is saying is that you're lucky to have such a big breakfast, when millions starved to death here during the potato famine," Mom translates. To Mrs. O'Reilly, she says, "Vivien hasn't had the benefit of my exposure to different cultures and dialects."

I treat myself to a private roll of the eyes as I dig into the fried eggs.

"Do you want a cuppa cha?" Mrs. O'Reilly asks me again, slowly and at full volume, as if speaking to someone with developmental delays. She waves the teapot under my nose.

Ah, I get it. "No thank you, I don't drink tea."

She frowns. "Coffee?"

I'm on a roll—I got that too. "Uh, no, just Mocha Frappaccinos."

She blinks at me uncomprehendingly, shaking her mop of tight, silver curls. Obviously Starbucks hasn't made it to sheep country yet.

"I've been thinking about what you said last night, Vivien," Mom says, checking over her shoulder to make sure Mrs. O'Reilly has left the kitchen before pushing the toast aside and reaching for her own cigarettes.

"About the lips?"

"No, not about the lips." She smiles at me indulgently. Clearly she's going to be tougher to irritate today. That's because she slept well, snoring away on the double bed, while I tossed and turned sleeplessly on the lumpy cot. "I mean about your calling me Annika. I think it might be fun."

"Fun?" I may be a little jet-lagged today, but something smells fishy and it isn't the blood pudding.

She flicks her monogrammed silver lighter and holds it to the cigarette's tip. "You know, more like pals."

"Pals," I repeat, noticing that it takes her three tries to light the cigarette. She inhales and leans toward me, oddly animated. Unless there's more than caffeine in her system, I'd say she's nervous. "You want to pretend we're pals?"

"Better yet, *sisters.* Why don't we say we're sisters on set?"

"I don't know, it sounds confusing to me." Not to mention ridiculous.

"Not at all, I'm an actress. That means you have the stage in your blood too."

"I doubt it, I take after Dad. Besides, Grandma would kill me."

Her expression darkens. "Grandma Reid? Yes, I guess she would, but acting isn't something one chooses, it's ordained." She pours more tea into her lipstick-smudged cup and asks, "What do you think of my plan?"

I think it sucks. It's not like I expected her to fall all over me in a frenzy of maternal adoration, but still . . . The whole age obsession is getting in the way of her common sense. On the other hand, why waste that angst if I can turn it to my advantage? I tally the pros and cons in my head before answering:

- My mother doesn't want to admit to anyone that I'm her daughter. *Con.*
- I won't have to admit to anyone that she's my mother. *Pro.*
- I'll be protecting her skinny, aging butt. *Con.*
- She will owe me because I'm protecting her skinny, aging butt. *Pro.*
- I can get something out of this. *Pro.*

Well, that's settled. "Okay, I'll call you Annika, but only if you call me Leigh."

"I suppose I could," she says, eyeing me warily. "At least on set."

I put my fork down, feeling the first faint stirrings of power within me. "Great! You know what would be even better? If you didn't smoke, at least inside. And could you talk to Mrs. O'Reilly about smoking in the cottage, too? Secondhand smoke kills, in case you've missed the commercials."

Her eyes narrow to slits as she takes a long, slow drag. I pick up a strip of bacon with my fingers and smile at her sweetly, certain that victory is at hand. She takes the cigarette between her forefinger and thumb and grinds it forcefully into the ashtray. Then she raises her eyebrows and demands, "Well?"

All hail the mighty Leigh! I should run for student body president next year. "You know, Annika, I was thinking—"

"Vivien," she interrupts. "Don't push your luck."

"Leigh," I say, already regretting that I wasted my shot on smoking, of all things. I should have held out for something big, like getting sent home early.

"Fine, *Leigh*." She subsides into silence to finish her tea. Several times her fingers twitch in the general direction of the cigarette package, but she resists. Instead, she pulls a tube of Channel Glazed Poppy lipstick out of the pocket of her Juicy Couture sweats and applies it expertly, without a mirror. "Let's go, darling," she says at last. "We're due on set in an hour."

"I doubt you'd call your sister 'darling,' Annika."

"I call everyone 'darling,' darling. Now, would you like to bring Greta along?"

"I told you, I do *not* play with dolls!"

She smiles again, showing the tips of her pretty eye teeth. "Relax, sweetie. I just thought you could show her off to the rest of the cast."

I see she isn't going down without a fight. Well neither am I. "By the way," I say, "I know it says 'Ann' on your birth certificate."

★   ★   ★

My *real* mother is probably a heavy-set, antisocial brunette who loves animals. Annika Anderson could never have produced me. We are *nothing* alike. The only logical explanation is that she hired a surrogate—someone she could pay to give up wine, smokes, and starvation for nine months. Although, come to think of it, prenatal exposure to wine, smokes, and starvation could explain my moodiness.

Since matching beauty marks aren't that noteworthy, I'm surprised when Colleen, the second assistant director on Mom's film, comments, "You're the spitting image of Annika."

The two of us are walking toward Mom's trailer but her words stop me in my tracks. "Time for new contacts, Colleen," I say.

She laughs. "I'm not having you on. You're so much alike, it's hard to believe you're just sisters." I look at her quickly. Mom delivered the introductions with more dramatic flair than I've noticed in her films but maybe Colleen is already onto us.

"That's because we're *not* just sisters," I say, "we're identical twins. But Annika's had some work done so that she could get more mature parts."

Colleen laughs again. "Well, you're funnier than Annika, that's for sure."

"Thanks." I suddenly feel a lot better about being here.

Although she must be in her early twenties, Colleen could pass for a student in my school. She has red hair and freckles and is wearing cargo pants, a T-shirt, and a baseball cap. Since her Irish accent is nowhere near as thick as Mrs. O'Reilly's, I can understand her perfectly. "You have the same smile and the same complexion," she continues. "And more than that, it's your mannerisms."

I can feel my face getting hot, but I try to keep my voice level. "How could I have her smile when *my* lips are real? I look like anybody else more than Annika."

"Well, I'd be thrilled if someone told me I looked like Annika Anderson," she says. "What's the matter, don't you two get along?"

"I'm fifteen, I don't get along with anybody. At least, according to my father."

Colleen is still laughing when she stops beside an enormous trailer.

"*This* is Annika's?"

"Why so surprised?"

"Her trailers are usually the size of a broom closet."

"Well, Paramount Studios doesn't skimp."

I still don't understand. As far as I know, my mother has only had big roles in small movies or small roles in big movies; this trailer is too classy for a bit-part actor. "Did she pull some favors to get it?"

Colleen slaps my arm gently. "Don't be mean. Annika's in a lead role and *Danny Boy* is the biggest film we've had in Dublin for a while." She unlocks the trailer and holds the door open for me. "Now, get some rest, you must be melted," she says. "I'll come and get you at lunch."

The trailer's common area includes a kitchen that is easily the size of the one in Grandma's "adult living" condo. I peek into the cupboards and find that they are stocked with every conceivable type of food, all of it untouched, since my mother never eats. Grabbing a bag of chocolate biscuits, I throw myself onto the couch and reach for the *Danny Boy* script on the glass coffee table in front of me. One day it will wing its way to Seattle with a personal note from the star: *"Vivien"* (scratched out). *"Leigh, so glad you could witness the making of this epic. It's the centerpiece of your collection."* I'll display it proudly with the rest, in a cardboard box in the basement.

Mom didn't say which role she is playing and I'm twenty pages into the script before I figure it out. After all, there's no demon lover, no vixen, no tramp. Instead, *Danny Boy* is the tale of a woman who makes good in New York and returns to her Irish hometown to find the son she gave up for adoption nineteen years before.

So that's why she's so anxious: Annika Anderson is playing a mother for the first time in her career (not to mention her life). It signals the end of an era as far as her acting goes. From temptress and lover to someone's mother . . . I'm surprised she took the role, but it is obviously a feature film as opposed to a made-for-TV movie and the script is better than the usual crap she does. It's an interesting story and the characters are likable. I suppose she thinks it's an opportunity to prove that she's a serious actor. Well, maybe she's got what it takes, but I wouldn't bet my allowance on it.

I read another thirty pages before the parallels to real life hit me: a mother trying to reunite with the kid she left years ago. Well, she'd better not get any big ideas about healing the rift with *me*. I am only here because Dad forced me to come and I have no intention of allowing life to imitate art. She's welcome to her midlife crisis, if that's what this is, but I want no part of a family reunion.

Throwing the script on the couch in disgust, I reach for a plastic toolbox that holds every pricey beauty product that's ever graced the pages of *In Style* magazine. In other words, a dream come true. Not that I've worn much makeup since Glen Myers dumped me. What's the point, when I know I will never love again? Not at J. D. Sandford Academy, at least. I've exhausted its romance potential. Being at a school for the academically gifted has certain disadvantages. For example, there's a much higher nerd-to-normal ratio than a regular high school offers. Being the lead singer in his own band, Glen was the coolest guy in the school.

How a nondescript girl with a healthy BMI won the heart of the coolest guy at J. D. Sandford is a subject of much debate between Abby and me. We've concluded that it's because I managed, through Abby's constant coaching, to look confident during the long pursuit prior to our first date. The only problem was that when I was alone with Glen, I became totally paralyzed, unable to do more than stare at him in awed disbelief. He made a few feeble attempts at conversation, but mostly we just made out in silence. We even broke up silently. At the Halloween dance, I went to the school washroom to spritz on more Liquid Sugar perfume, and came back to find Glen engaged in lively banter with Madison Farnsworth. They were talking so hard they didn't even notice me, so I slipped out the door with Abby and cried all the way home. I never heard from him again. At school on Monday, I pretended not to recognize him in the hall and he did the same. It was beyond brutal.

Selecting some products from Mom's toolbox, I head into the trailer's dim bathroom. Even though some of the bulbs around the makeup mirror have burned out, I can see that I have another thing in common with my mother: I am very pale. No need to resort to blood pudding, however, when there's a tube of tanning cream in my hand. I apply it generously. After that I try covering the beauty mark with some concealer, but it looks even more prominent somehow, so I add some blush. Then I play with half a dozen shades of eye shadow before reaching for a tube of Glazed Poppy lipstick. The look isn't great—even I can see that—but I've definitely matured by a couple of years. I should seize the moment and hitchhike into Dublin to get that tattoo.

Instead, I take a nap and I'm still asleep when Colleen opens the door and calls, "Lunchtime, Sleeping Beauty." I step groggily into the gray afternoon light and Colleen does a double take. "I see you found your ma's makeup."

"Oh right," I say, remembering. Then, *"Hey, how'd you know she's my mother?"*

Grinning, Colleen says, "A good guess that you just confirmed. I suspected when you got so mad over my saying you look like Annika. It reminded me about how I felt about *my* mother at your age—still feel about her, matter of fact."

"Really?"

"Oh yeah. She's right narky half the time. And I'm right narky the other half."

"Is narky . . . ?"

"Bitchy? Yeah." She throws her arm around my shoulders. "Why don't we let Annika think everyone buys the sister act?"

"Playing a mother must be freaking her out."

"It probably is, but this is a great opportunity for her. The film business is so hard on mature actresses. The last one I worked with only allowed one side of her face to be filmed and flew a hair and makeup team with her everywhere."

We arrive on set to find Annika perched in her director's chair while a dark-haired guy hovers over her. Sighting me, she bolts out of her chair, exclaiming, "My god, what have you done!"

"Nothing, why?"

"Your face, your face." She's almost moaning.

"I tried some of your makeup, no big deal."

"You're covered in streaks." She grabs my chin, her fake nails digging into my skin. When I reach up to pull her hand away, she gasps in horror. "Look at your palms! You've been into my tanning cream!"

"Relax, I'll go wash it off." I try to sound cool but the sight of my orange palms alarms me. What must my face look like?

"It doesn't wash off for days."

"Days?"

"This is a disaster," my mother continues. I turn helplessly to Colleen, who's covering her mouth with her hand. Mom lays into her too. "Well, I'm glad *you* can see the humor in this, Colleen. You were supposed to be watching her."

"I don't need a babysitter," I say.

"Clearly you do," Mom says. Her eyes are icy.

"Calm yourself, Annika," Colleen intervenes. "We'll take Leigh to the makeup department and let them work their magic."

"Good idea," Mom says, brightening.

The dark-haired guy, who has watched the exchange in silence, steps forward. He looks to be around twenty and he's the best-looking man I have ever, *ever* seen. Maybe I was a little too hasty in giving up on love. Compared to this guy, Glen Myers is a pathetic excuse for manhood. I have just come face-to-face with perfection.

"How about lunch, ladies?" he says. "I'm so hungry I could eat a baby's arse through the bars of a cot."

Okay, so nobody's perfect. Still, his accent is just like Colin Farrell's and he's even better looking. For one thing, he is taller, which matters since I was five foot nine last time I checked. For another, he has the most gorgeous blue eyes imaginable.

"Can't you see we have a crisis on our hands?" my mother asks him. She tries to pull me away, but it's as if my feet are stuck to the floor.

He smiles at me with brilliant white teeth before turning to my mother. "Well, aren't you going to introduce me, Annie? I am your son, after all."

My mother glowers at him. "That's not funny, Sean. It's a *role*."

"I'm Sean," he says, holding out his hand to me. "Annie's illegitimate child."

Annie's fierce expression dissuades me from mentioning that I am her legitimate one. Instead, I take his hand and gaze into his eyes. They are so blue that my mother's seem colorless by comparison. "I'm Leigh," I say, "Annie's sister."

His smile widens until it blocks out everything else in the studio. "Ah," he says, "the *orange* sheep of the family."

I pull my hand back in mortification. Colleen jumps to my defense. "You can't blame a girl for trying to get a little color in this climate."

"The blushing should help," he says.

"Stop acting the maggot, Sean Finlay," Colleen says. "Go get yourself some lunch now."

He swaggers off and I stare after him until my mother yanks on my arm again.

A long-lost brother. This could turn out to be a happy family reunion after all.

four

They call him the Lord of the Brush. As the Oscar-winning head of the hair and makeup department, Finian Doyle commands a lot of respect on set—especially from my mother. She first worked with Finian years ago and speaks of him in such reverent tones that I've made it my personal mission in life to despise him. I suspect it won't be hard to do when he sweeps into the makeup trailer wearing a flowing purple caftan. There's a scrawny gray ponytail stretching down his back and half a dozen long, beaded necklaces around his neck, including one with an elaborate Celtic cross. At best, the man is an aging hippy; at worst he's a druid. Either way, I don't like the way he looks at me while he arranges his homemade potions ceremonially on the vanity, as if I'm a blank slate waiting to be transformed for the big screen. I don't care what Mom says: if there's incense or chanting, I'm outta here.

Bracelets jangling, Lord Finian lifts my chin with his finger and tilts my face this way and that while observing me carefully through silver-rimmed half-glasses. Looking down to avoid his gaze, I notice that his robe touches the floor. He's hiding something under there. Like hooves. Maybe he gallops into the hills by night in search of toadstools to use in his signature age-defying face mask. At any rate, it's quite clear that while Finian Doyle may be revered in the film business as some kind of a hero, in the real world, he qualifies as a wacko.

"Well, then," he says, releasing my chin, "you're a beautiful girl."

I suppose there's no reason to question his sanity just yet. Keeping an open mind is a sign of maturity.

As he runs his hand along a row of creams, I notice an intricate blue tattoo on his ring finger. "A wedding ring tattoo," I say. "Cool."

"The lover's knot," he acknowledges in his lilting Irish accent. "It would be cooler if mine hadn't chucked me, though. I was a crazy romantic cub in those days. You know how it is when you think you've found the boy of your dreams." I nod, trying to look worldly. "Anyway, you aren't here to listen to me rabbit on about my love life—let's get down to business. Those orange streaks are sooooo last year!"

My mother sighs despondently in the makeup chair beside mine. "Can you fix her, Fin?"

"She's not a broken down lorry, Annika," he says. "But both of you will be purring like kittens when my work here is done. After all, glorious skin runs in the family."

My mother practically wriggles with joy. She is so ashamed of how I look that she has actually agreed to surrender her claim on Finian and allow his goofy assistants, Mary and Maude, to prepare her for the day's shoot.

"Sponge?" Mary asks, holding out her hand, palm up, to Maude.

"Sponge!" Maude slaps a sponge into Mary's outstretched hand.

"Powder?"

"Powder!"

And so on.

"Isn't this exciting?" My mother beams at me in the enormous, brightly lit mirror that runs the length of the trailer. "Your first make-over."

"Totally." But I refuse to show any enthusiasm. I am here only because she put her foot down: I must report to hair and makeup every morning until my fake tan fades or stay at the cottage with scary Mrs. O'Reilly. Since the cottage's quaint features include ancient wiring that could blow my laptop to pieces, that isn't an option. This country is barely civilized.

"It's a rite of passage for any girl," Mom continues, leaning back in her chair with an expression of sheer bliss.

"Yeah, it's a spiritual journey all right."

Mom turns to Finian: "She gets the attitude from her father—I mean *our* father."

"Nice try, Baby Doll," he says. "Finian sees and knows all: this clever girl is your daughter."

My mother's expression makes me laugh out loud. She drops the sister act immediately. "Well, she's not clever enough to appreciate the importance of a good complexion." To me, she adds, "Watch and learn, young lady. This man can change your life."

"What she *means,* is that feeling good about how you look will give you confidence and *that* can change your life. You're perfect just the way you are."

I'm tempted to fake a gag, just to prove I haven't been totally bewitched, but I suppress it. With Sean on the scene, there's no harm in looking my best. "Can you do anything about this mole, Finian?" I ask, pointing to the beast on my cheek.

"It's a beauty mark," Mom answers for him. "Don't touch it."

"Annika's is sprouting hair," I say. "Grab your hedge clippers, Mary."

My mother starts to rise in her seat, enraged. Finian turns quickly and eases her back down with a hand on her shoulder. "Take deep, even breaths," he tells her. She sinks into a silent sulk.

Shaking a finger at me, he slides a CD into his futuristic stereo and starts singing along with J-Lo: *"Let's get loud, let's get loud."* The makeup trailer is rocking and despite my efforts to remain detached, I'm enjoying myself. Fin buffs and plucks and polishes to the beat for another twenty minutes before turning me to face the mirror.

"Wow!" I say, staring at my reflection with eyes that are no longer muddy, but green. My hair has gone from stringy to swingy. Even the mole looks smaller, somehow. In fact, if Glen Myers saw me now, he'd realize that there's more to romance than clever conversation. Still, it will likely take stronger magic than Fin's to banish the first impression I made on Sean yesterday. "Do you think I could pass for eighteen?"

"Remember wanting to look older, Annika?" he says, dodging the question. "Now we spend all our time trying to look younger."

Annika frowns, clearly not amused at being grouped in the geriatric category. Her pleasure at my transformation outweighs her irritation, however, because she sends Maude to wardrobe to find something I can borrow to complete the look. "No cleavage," she decrees. This is rich, coming from a woman whose body is regularly on display for all of North America to see. Since when did she discover maternal instincts?

Returning with an armload of T-shirts, a suede jacket, and pair of platform sandals that are miraculously my size, Maude says, "Okay, Cinderella, let's see how you look in this."

As we walk to set, Mom says, "You really do look fabulous, darling."

I can see that she means it and that annoys me. It's like I've been sucked into her world in two days without putting up a fight. "You call me 'darling' to avoid calling me Leigh. It's cheating."

"I have the shakes from nicotine withdrawal right now so don't talk to me about cheating."

"Well, don't get used to this look because I'm not going to be one of those high-maintenance women." My mother, who is at the top of the high-maintenance category, looks taken aback. I press my advantage. "You just wanted me to look older because it's more believable that we're sisters."

"If you go through life imagining slights, you'll end up a miserable woman."

Before I can reply, we reach the set, where Roger Knelman, the director, is pacing. My mother fluffs her hair and hurries toward him. There's a spring in her step that he doesn't seem to warrant. Sure, he's a successful director, even I know that, but he's no Sean Finlay. In fact, in his limp corduroy pants and plaid shirt, he looks like a troll. I hope Annika doesn't think this is the best she can do.

"Roger," she trills, waving her ruby fingertips, "come say hello to my sister."

Up close, Roger isn't quite as bad. He's shorter than my mother and me, but he has a nice enough smile. The lines around his eyes make him look tired, but they also suggest he could be funny if he were in the right mood. I don't like his glasses, though. They have dark, heavy frames and the lenses are so thick that his brown eyes look huge and bulbous.

Roger takes my hand and holds it while looking me over from head to foot. It's a little odd, but I give him the benefit of the doubt. Maybe he evaluates everyone for screen potential. I try to pull my hand away, but he puts his other hand on top of it in a vice. Okay, that's just plain creepy. There's a little flutter of panic in my stomach and I can't help wondering if Mom was thinking of Roger when she nixed the cleavage. "Well, well, she's the bashful type, is she?"

"She's the *jail-bait* type, Roger." Mom's smile vanishes. I expect she's regretting the make-over right about now.

"Don't be jealous," he says, releasing my hand and taking hers. "You're still my leading lady. But there's always a young babe nipping at your heels in this business."

"Not *this* young babe." Mom leads me to her director's chair. "Sit here and stay out of Roger's way," she whispers.

"That guy is a pig," I say.

"That guy is my boss," she cautions me. "You must be polite."

"Just don't leave me alone with him, Annika, or I'll grind that troll into the Irish soil with my new heels." More likely, I'll run crying to Colleen as fast as these platform shoes can carry me.

Sean's arrival on set cuts our exchange short. The air in the studio suddenly becomes carbonated, all prickly and effervescent in my lungs. Time slows down.

Scene 6: Leigh and Sean Meet Again

Their eyes lock as he crosses the studio toward her. She reads the admiration on his face. Yesterday she seemed like a child to him, but today he sees her as she really is: a beautiful woman. He reaches for her hand.

SEAN
Leigh, you look so mature.

LEIGH
Well, I am eighteen, Sean.

SEAN
What a relief, gorgeous, because I dreamed about you last night.

LEIGH
[giggling flirtatiously, à la Annika]
You did?

SEAN
[pulling Leigh closer to him]
I haven't been able to get you off my mind since we met.

LEIGH
I've thought about you too.

```
                    SEAN
       [wrapping his arms around Leigh]
       My sweet, sweet Leigh, let's not waste this
       precious time talking.
```

The real Sean's voice cuts into my thoughts as he saunters across the studio toward us. "Who's your lovely friend, Annie?"

Rapture and despair in equal parts overtake me: we met only eighteen hours ago and he doesn't even recognize me; on the other hand, he thinks I'm lovely.

Rolling her eyes, my mother sighs, "Sean, you met Leigh yesterday."

"Right, the orange kid," he says, smirking. "I hardly recognized you."

"I'm not a kid," I mutter.

Sean turns back to my mother, ignoring me. "Yer man Finian's been waving his wand, has he, Annie? Well, he did a cracking job, so he did. She's like one of those 'before' and 'after' adverts."

I'm still trying to think of a brilliant response when Roger calls, "We're ready, everyone."

The scene they're shooting today takes place right after my mother's character, Fiona, introduces herself to her long-lost son, Danny. She's returned to her hometown from New York, found the family that raised him, and invited him to a pub, where they have their first real conversation. It's supposed to be an awkward and bittersweet meeting. He feigns indifference, but she is already beginning to realize what she gave up.

Danny Boy, Scene 19

The regulars are lined up along the bar at Gallagher's, the local pub. Fiona and Danny are sitting in

a booth. Danny tips half a pint of Guinness down his
throat, wipes his mouth with the back of his hand, and
stares at the television above the bar. Fiona sips the
black Irish beer and grimaces. In the background, a
fiddle plays. She reaches out to touch Danny's arm.

                         FIONA
          So, here we are.

"Cut!" Roger yells. "Any stiffer, Annika, and we'd be calling a
coroner. This is the son you abandoned as an infant. Now you're
seeing him as a strapping young man. Can we have a little feeling?"

Mom looks stunned. She closes her eyes, opens them again,
and in a throaty purr, says, "So, here we are."

"Cut! Jesus, Annika, not *that* kind of feeling. This is a family
picture."

I sink a little lower in my chair. Flirtation comes so naturally to
her that I don't think she even knows she's doing it—or how to
turn it off. No wonder she's never landed a major role before. It's
not like I had delusions of her theatrical genius, but this is worse
than I thought. And her Irish accent is totally lame.

"Again!" Roger yells. "And . . . rolling."

Taking a deep breath, Mom forces an animated smile: "So, here
we are!"

"*Cut!* Tell me that isn't perkiness! It's a serious moment, Annika. Again."

Leaning her chin on her hand and gazing at Sean, Mom injects
so much seriousness into her tone that it comes out sounding tear-
drenched. "So, here we are."

"*Cut!* How about saving some emotion for your next line?"

Like Goldilocks, she's either too hot or too cold. Taking a deep
breath, she tries one more time: "So, here we are."

"Enough!" Roger shouts. He storms over to the booth and

waves the script under my mother's nose. "I realize this is a stretch after the *Passionate Hearts* series, but my god, woman, you're displaying the range of an iguana."

Sean stands and puts a hand on Roger's shoulder. "Relax, man, it's only one line."

"Only one line! Are you an idiot? This is their first conversation alone. It's one of the most important lines in the script." Mom is staring at Roger silently, her blue eyes wide and confused. I recognize she's in that place where you know no matter where you step, you're going down. I've been there myself. Turning to her, Roger says with mock patience, "Why don't you tell me what you're trying to do with this line? What are you feeling?"

Colleen, who has silently come up behind me, puts her hand on my shoulder.

"He's *horrible!*" I whisper savagely. "Why does she let him treat her like that?"

"He's the director," Colleen says simply. "Maybe it's a strategy for getting the right performance out of her."

I worry he's being mean because she gave him a hard time about me earlier, but I'm not about to share this theory with Colleen.

Sean, who hasn't learned his lesson, says, "Why don't we take five and give Annie a chance to think about her motivation?"

Roger turns without another word and storms off the set.

"Wow, that was so *nice* of Sean," I say, noticing that my voice sounds squeaky.

"That was so *stupid* of Sean," Colleen corrects me. "Roger will make him pay."

Surprisingly, my mother doesn't look any too pleased with Sean either. For some reason, she didn't want to be rescued. When he leans across the table and puts his hand on her shoulder, she pulls away and starts flipping through her script.

Sean slides out of the booth and pours himself a cup of tea at the snack table. Before I even realize I'm moving, I find myself standing beside him. It's like he exerts some sort of gravitational pull. I examine the cookies, trying to look casual. Any minute now, I will say something impressive and dazzle him with my wit. I'm just waiting for inspiration to strike.

"Try the fly cemetery," he suggests.

I stare into his eyes, transfixed, before offering this conversational gem: "What?"

"The currant buns," he says, pointing at them. "Young 'uns always love 'em."

This is too much. You'd think he was my mother's age, the way he carries on. My face flushes and I practically spit out the words: "I am not a child."

"Come on, you're a babby—still wet behind the ears."

"I am *not* a baby!" Furious, I put my hands on my hips and stomp one platform heel so hard I nearly tip over.

He laughs. "Of course you're not. Sorry, luv."

"Leigh, I need your help," says Colleen, arriving in time to prevent further humiliation. "We're changing tomorrow's start time and I've got to rubberstamp a million sheets of paper. Can you give us a hand?"

★   ★   ★

The stamping provides a good outlet for my frustrations. *Thunk! Thunk!*

"You'll break your wrist at that rate," Colleen says, looking up from her computer.

Still stamping, I say, "I've got to prove to Sean that I'm not a kid." *Thunk!*

"Steady on there, Lover Girl. Sean's quite a boyo."

"I can handle it—*Thunk! Thunk!*—I'm practically seventeen."

"Really? You said fifteen yesterday."

"Well, who's counting?"

"Your mother, most likely."
Let's hope Annie's math skills are as strong as her acting.

```
Abs,
Sean iz d cutest guy eva
& so nice. At least, he's
nice 2 Annika. He's goin 2 b
a huge star, I cn teL.
L
```

```
L,
Kewl! An Irish movie star
bf. That's amazn.
How old iz he?
A
```

Does everyone in the world have an age fixation?

```
Abs,
Not sure, mAbE 19.
But I tink he finds me
mature 4 my age.
L
```

five

The single weak ray of sunshine breaking through the clouds has addled my mother's brain. There is no other possible explanation for her announcement that we will be spending a perfectly good Sunday afternoon hiking through the glens near Bray.

I expected to visit Dublin this weekend, but Annika—exhausted from her week of blowing scenes—spent virtually all of Saturday sleeping, a black mask over her eyes. Periodically, she emerged from the bedroom to stand shivering on the doorstep in her silk pajamas, a cigarette in her hand. I spent the day huddled beside an electric heater with a book, wondering why I had to come so far to do exactly what I'd be doing at home, only in less comfort. Of course, at home, Dad would be preparing meals that target all the food groups, whereas Mrs. O'Reilly has a different approach to nutrition. She prepared the usual greasy breakfast, a cold lunch of bread and pale fried meat, and returned—still wearing her ratty bathrobe—to fry up meat and potatoes for dinner. My vegan ambitions have rolled over and died.

The hike is probably the result of a long-distance mind-meld with Jared, Mom's personal trainer, who is currently surfing off the coast of Baja. Jared made her promise to stay active during the Irish shoot, so that they wouldn't have to start from scratch when she gets back. With so little flesh to cover them, Mom has to keep her muscles well toned.

Dad and I used to go on camping trips every summer, but lately I haven't done anything more strenuous than stroll around a mall. Not that I'm about to admit that to Nature Girl. "Sounds great," I say, meeting her eyes squarely. If she can hike, I can hike.

After a ninety-minute prep session that may or may not have included a nap, she returns wearing a powder blue Gor-Tex outfit, complete with waterproof hat and hiking boots. Finally we step out the door, only to find that the single ray of sunshine has given up the fight against the clouds, and a wall of mist is drifting up the road from the coast. Undeterred, Mom pulls her sunglasses out of her pocket. "Isn't this lovely?" she asks, sucking in a lungful of fog.

"Lovely," I agree. A slight drizzle is starting to fall, so I zip up the yellow raincoat I found hanging on the cottage's back door. "There's no place I'd rather be."

"Always so sarcastic, Vivien . . . Why not look on the bright side for a change?"

She's taken to calling me Vivien again since we left the film set. I've been letting it ride because she continues to step outside before she lights up.

"I can't see the bright side through the fog. Can I borrow your shades?"

"Darling, the air is so fresh and clear here. Smell those wild-flowers!"

"All I smell is sheep dung."

"And that bracing breeze," she says, stepping briskly along the dirt road. "So energizing!"

As we pass Mrs. O'Reilly's cottage, her shaggy sheepdog, Skip, dashes through the gate toward us, tail wagging furiously. Smiling, I struggle to pat his head as he leaps around me. Wet dog: now there's a smell I like. I've been desperately dog-sick this week for

Millie, my West Highland terrier. She's staying with Grandma Reid while I'm away since Dad is in a busy stretch at work. Grandma wasn't too thrilled about it either, because Millie, who's barely a year old, is quite a handful. Then there's the matter of Percival, Grandma's grumpy, old Persian cat.

"Don't touch that thing, Vivien," Mom says, looking at Skip disapprovingly. "You don't know where it's been."

"Him. Skip's a boy." I deliberately lean down to let him lick my face.

Mom gasps in horror. She hates animals. In fact, as soon as she moved to L.A., Dad made a point of buying a cocker spaniel, whom he named Delores after Mom's mother, Grandma Anderson. My other, nicer Grandma found this very funny at the time, he says, having met Delores (the human). When we named Millie after Great-aunt Mildred, however, Grandma Reid was less amused. "Just what am I supposed to say to Aunt Millie?" she demanded. But Aunt Millie, age ninety-seven, is probably long past caring.

Skip runs over to Mom and shoves his snout where it doesn't belong. "Back off, you little beast," she says, removing her rain hat and swatting him with it. "Go home."

"Let him come, Mom, he'll keep the killer sheep away."

"Killer sheep? That's ridiculous." But she lets her sunglasses slide down her nose to get a good look at me.

"I'm just telling you what the local newspaper says. Sheep rabies is on the rise here."

"I don't believe you."

I shrug. "If it's in *Bray People,* it must be true. They keep referring to you as the 'famous American actress,' by the way."

Pushing her glasses into place against the cruel glare, she says, "Fine, bring the dog, but if I end up with muddy paw prints on these pants, you'll be doing the laundry."

The rain is coming down in sheets by the time we reach the outskirts of town and find a narrow dirt path into the hills. Skip, racing ahead of us toward Glencree, is a black-and-white blur.

"This is what I miss in Hollywood," she shouts back over her shoulder. "*Real* weather."

I snort. The rain is pricking at my face like needles and my favorite Guess jeans are soaked to the knee. With the treads on my sneakers full of mud, I'm sliding all over the path. Thanks to her fancy new hiking boots, Mom is now far ahead of me. I refuse to give up, however. The woman didn't own running shoes until she turned forty: she'll crumble. Already there's less talk of "bracing breezes." Or maybe it's getting swallowed by the elements.

At the top of a hill, she stops to watch Skip, who is bringing in a herd of sheep from the field. Barking crazily, he circles them, forcing them forward until they surge across the path between us. It's the coolest thing I've ever seen, but it's lost on Mom. Squealing, she backs into a stone wall, her powder blue arms flailing. She takes off her hat again and waves it at the sheep closest to her. "I think this one is the leader."

"Try singing. Mrs. O'Reilly says it calms them."

Sadly, my mother doesn't take the bait. Instead, she gives the lead sheep a hard whack with the hat. It reaches out to grab her sleeve with its teeth. Her scream is blood-curdling (I heard it first in her demon-temptress role).

"Do something!" She sounds a little panicky now. "It's attacking me!"

"He probably just wants an autograph." I turn and call Skip. "Off! Off!" I tell him, sweeping my arm toward the field the way I've seen farmers do it in documentaries. He gets the general idea from my gestures and starts herding the sheep away.

Rubbing her wrist where the sheep gnawed at her Gor-Tex, Mom grumbles, "I don't want to hear about this on set, tomorrow, Vivien."

"Leigh," I correct her, leading the way back to the cottage so that she can't see my grin.

★ ★ ★

The next morning, it's a relief to be back on set. I'm happy to see Colleen and Finian and even happier to see Sean. Over the weekend, I had plenty of opportunity to master my feelings for him and I am confident that I am in full control. Last week, I was simply overwhelmed by his good looks. It was infatuation, pure and simple. This week I am thinking rationally.

I've decided I need a strategy to get to know him, since my first approach was a disaster. I'm going to figure out how to walk before I run. I'll start with the conversational basics and build. Today, I'll tackle pleasantries, such as "How are you?" or "How was your weekend?"

I have my chance after several crappy takes of the day's first scene. Sean, I am sorry to say, keeps flubbing his lines.

"Hope you weren't watching that holy show," he says, arriving beside me at the craft table, which holds a constant supply of food and drink for the cast and crew. Picking up a scone, he bites off almost half and mumbles through it, "I did it all arseways."

My new strategy relies on both of us using regular English, but I try just the same. "How was your weekend?" I ask, handing him a serviette. I can forgive his bad eating habits. He's probably just in a hurry to get back on set. Besides, you've got to trap the beast before you can tame it.

"Ah, I was rubber last night," he replies, shaking his head. "Totally scuttered. Paying for it today."

No more enlightened than before, I attempt another basic phrase. "That's interesting."

Stuffing the remaining half of the scone into his mouth, he raises his eyebrows at me. "If you think so, you and Annie should come along sometime."

I have no idea what he's talking about, but it sounds like he's practically asking me out. The new approach must be working. "We'd love to," I say.

He winks at me. "You talk Annie into it then."

Tracking Colleen down in her office, I say, "Sean just invited my mother and me to go scuttering."

"Pardon me?"

"He said he was rubber and scuttered last night and that we should join him sometime."

"Jaysus, Leigh, that means he was drunk off his head," she says, shaking her head in disgust. "It's not something anyone should have to witness."

My feelings for Sean must be maturing beyond mere infatuation, because this information doesn't faze me. Last week, I thought he was nearly perfect, but this week, I've accepted that there are many sides to him, some more likable than others.

It's like what Grandma Reid said when I complained about Stan the Garbageman picking his teeth with his Home Depot credit card: "Nobody is perfect, but when you really love somebody, you have to accept the weaknesses with the strengths." She reminded me that Stan cooks dinner every night and brings her flowers twice a week.

I guess it's okay for Sean to blow off steam now and again. He's a complicated man. I can tell that from the way he sits in his director's chair staring into space, pondering the mysteries of the universe. What he needs is a calm, patient woman to love and understand him.

That would be me.

★　★　★

Sean is standing beside the craft table shouting, it seems, at no one in particular.

"Is that all we get around here: bloody scones, morning, noon, and night? It never bloody well ends. Let's start measuring time in scones, why don't we? It's half-past scones already, so could we get some real food? A man can't work on scones alone."

The production manager hurries over and offers to get Sean

anything he likes. Noticing me watching, Sean winks again and places an order for fish and chips.

"Haddock, not cod!" he calls after the production manager. "Batter extra crispy!"

Clearly he's giving what Colleen calls his "inner diva" a workout. Every actor has one, she says. Annika sure does. Just the same, tantrums aren't becoming and I must help him fix his bad habits. Not that it worked for Grandma: when she confiscated Stan's Home Depot card, he started using his Visa card to pick his teeth instead.

Sean will love me enough to change. I will set him a good example by showing my high standards at all times. I will be a model of class and virtue.

★ ★ ★

"Give us a light, Annie," Sean says, sitting down beside my mother at lunch and offering her one of his cigarettes.

"I don't smoke inside," she replies, looking at me pointedly. "Do I, Leigh?"

"No, Annika, you don't," I say.

"Leigh thinks smoking is disgusting," she tells Sean as he reaches for the matches on the next table.

Lighting his cigarette, he deliberately sends a gust of smoke across the table at me. "Does she, now?"

"I'm just concerned about your health, Annika," I say. "You're not getting any younger."

Mom scowls at me, picks up her tea, and stalks off toward the makeup trailer, leaving me alone with Sean. I couldn't have planned this better.

"So you don't smoke," he says.

This is our chance to connect as two adults and I don't want to mess it up by sounding too prissy. There will be time to impress him with my virtue later. "Oh, I smoke now and then."

"That's like saying you breathe now and then," he says, getting up to leave himself. "You either do or you don't."

"I'm trying to quit," I call after him.

I should have stuck with asking about his weekend.

★　★　★

Grandma's text message arrives in the afternoon. I told her to call me, but she really wants to be "with it." I appreciate her good intentions, but her messages go on forever. I scroll through quickly, looking for news of Millie. Oh-oh. Grandma woke up to chunks of orange fluff all over the house this morning. Happily, Percival, who happens to be orange, was found alive and well behind the refrigerator. Grandma can't type fast enough to describe at length how she really feels about this. After all, she has to save her strength for reminding me to dress warmly and be polite.

"Got a pen pal?" Sean asks, leaning over my shoulder.

I drop the phone into my backpack before he can read Grandma's suggestion that I count to ten before every comment I make to my mother. "It's from my ex-boyfriend," I offer, inspired to improvise. "I broke up with him before I left because he's too immature for me— even though he's almost nineteen. Now he's begging me to take him back."

"Bollocks," he says, grinning at me. "Annie told me you got sacked—that you're heartbroken and all that."

The world starts spinning around me. I hold on to the arms of the director's chair and wait for the nausea to pass.

Why didn't I let the sheep finish her off?

★　★　★

I've been hiding in the makeup trailer while my mother shoots a scene with Sean. A girl can only stand so much humiliation in one day.

"What you need," Finian says, after hearing my confession, "is a little help from the Blarney Stone."

"What's that?"

"A magical stone in Blarney Castle that gives you the gift of the gab. After you kiss it, you can sweet-talk kings. Wouldn't advise wasting it on an eejit like Sean, though."

"He's not an idiot," I retort hotly. "He's just . . . an idiot."

"Exactly," Fin says, patting my shoulder. "All men are."

"Except you."

"Some would say otherwise. Now, into the chair with you." He reaches for his brushes. Although my fake tan faded days ago, Fin still gives me a polish when he has the time. Today he twists my hair into an elaborate updo and pins it with sparkling clips. "You really must get out more," he says. "Too much time on a film set isn't good for anyone."

I tell him about my weekend, describing the hike in great detail. Fin has to put down his brush, he's laughing so hard.

"What's so funny?" my mother asks suspiciously, stepping into the trailer.

"Your daughter knows how to spin a yarn, that's all."

"Don't you have anything better to do than spin yarns?" Mom asks me, obviously still burned about my comment at lunch.

"Actually, I'm thinking about doing some sightseeing."

"Not alone, you're not," she snaps.

"Come on, Mom, I'm bored. There's nothing to do here but watch you. That got old real fast."

She looks at Finian helplessly. "What am I going to do with her?"

"I have an idea," he says. "You keep complaining that they didn't give you a personal assistant on this production, why don't you pay Leigh to help you?"

"How on earth could she help?"

"You have no idea how talented I am," I say. "You barely know me."

Fin interrupts smoothly. "She could run errands, make sure you have your script when you need it—get you organized."

"I haven't noticed any organizational skills," she says. "You should see the state of our bedroom."

I'm about to flounce off in a huff, but I reconsider. Mom hasn't been as generous with her cash as she usually is, which suggests she isn't feeling very guilty about me right now. It's probably time to back off a little.

"I can organize, Mom. I was student council treasurer last year."

Actually, Abby was treasurer, but my mother wouldn't know the difference. Besides, how hard can organizing her life be?

"Well, all right," she says, reluctantly, getting out of the chair after Fin's touch-up. "Let's give it a try. But no trips on your own."

"Thanks, Fin," I say, giving him a hug as Mom leaves. "I'm saving to get a tattoo."

"Are you now? Well, save for laser treatments to remove it while you're at it." He pulls up the sleeve of his caftan to reveal a faint green vine encircling the name "Kelly."

"Who's Kelly?"

"A mistake I made in my twenties that I remember every time I roll up my sleeve. I've spent six hundred euros so far trying to get rid of it."

"What about your lover's knot?" I ask. The tattooed ring on his finger is bright and vibrant still.

"Ah, but that wasn't for Kelly," he says, tracing it with his index finger. His eyes look a little misty, but he smiles. "I'm just a sentimental fool."

A wolverine might not be the best tattoo choice after all. It has to be something that will still make me smile when I get to be Fin's age.

six

My first assignment as personal assistant to film star Annika Anderson is to inventory her private makeup collection and note what's running low. I line up dozens of products on the trailer's dining table while my mother drapes herself on the couch to read. A love of novels is another thing I've apparently inherited from my mother, since my father only reads newspapers and magazines. Still, our taste in novels couldn't be more different. She's just started rereading *Persuasion*. Since I mentioned a few days ago that it's my least favorite Jane Austen novel, I suspect she's trying to start a debate. Well, I am not taking the bait. I have anti-aging creams to catalog.

Colleen knocks and pokes her head in the door. "I need you to do me a favor, Leigh."

"Sure," I say, already bored with life in the fast lane.

"We had cast a local teenager for a small part in *Danny Boy* and she's down with the flu. How about doing the read-through with us today?"

I'd rather stamp script changes or deliver paperwork for her. I'm curious about a lot of careers, but acting isn't one of them.

Before I can say so, Mom pipes up: "I'm sorry, Colleen, but Leigh isn't an actor."

"I know, Annika, but it's only a few lines. We just need a warm body."

"I wish I could spare her, but she's my personal assistant now. She has duties."

"It will take an hour at most."

"I flew Leigh here at my own expense because I really need support on this film."

Actually, my father flew me here at his expense and she knows I know it. Obviously, she really doesn't want me to do this. Which makes the idea a whole lot more appealing.

"I can catalog these creams later, Annika," I say. "I'd like to help Colleen."

"Roger will be pleased," Colleen says. "He suggested asking Leigh."

My mother gets to her feet. "Why didn't you say so? Take my script, darling."

"Now, wait a second," I say, changing my mind. I have no intention of pleasing that creep. "I'm too shy to read lines in front of people."

Colleen has come prepared for this: "Sean is in the scene. Maybe he can coach you."

I snatch the script from my mother's hand and trot after Colleen.

★ ★ ★

Roger's "office" is a motor home even bigger than Mom's. We enter through a kitchen that gleams with stainless steel cooking appliances, none of which look used.

Sean and Roger have taken over two of the four sofas in the living room, huge platters of fruit and cheese on the coffee table in front of them.

"Hi, girls," Roger says, sounding surprisingly friendly. Since our first meeting on set, he's totally ignored me, except to wave me aside if I'm in his way. "Get some food and pull up a sofa," he says, patting the seat beside him.

I take my time loading a plate so that Colleen has to sit down first. She takes the seat next to Roger, leaving me to stake out a place closer to Sean.

"Howya, Leigh," he says. "Not still pining for that American gack, I hope." Before I can reply, he reaches for the enormous teapot on the coffee table. "Cuppa tea, luv?"

I nod happily. Even though everybody calls everybody "luv" around here, I like the way it sounds when Sean says it. It's easy to imagine that he actually means it. Pouring milk into my tea, he adds a spoonful of sugar, somehow knowing without even asking just how I would like it if I drank tea. That's the type of connection we have.

Colleen explains that the scene we're rehearsing won't actually be shot for weeks. This read-through is supposed to show any problems with the dialogue so that the script doctors can fine-tune it.

"To bring you up to speed, Leigh, in this scene, Sean's character, Danny, and his half-sister, Sinead, are visiting their Aunt Jenny. I'll read Jenny's part and you'll read Sinead's. I've flagged your lines for you," Colleen adds, handing me several loose pages of script. "Danny will confess that he's thinking about leaving Ireland to stay with his birth mother, Fiona. Got all that?"

"I've read the script."

"Don't look so worried," Colleen says, leaning over to give my arm a squeeze. "It's just a read-through, you can't go wrong."

"Didn't you tell her about the talent scout eavesdropping from the bedroom?" Roger asks.

"He's kidding," she reassures me. "Okay, let's get started."

JENNY

It's good to see you, Danny. We've barely
heard a word from you since Fiona arrived
in Dublin.

Transforming instantly into Danny, Sean slouches sullenly on the couch.

> DANNY
>
> I've been busy.

> JENNY
>
> Spending all your time with *that woman*, I suppose.

Colleen tries to sound angry, but it's obvious why she spends her time *behind* the camera.

> DANNY
>
> Well, she *is* my mother. What do you expect?

> JENNY
>
> I expect you to remember that Kathleen is your real mother. Fiona may have given birth to you, but who changed your dirty nappies and wiped your snotty nose? Kathleen, that's who. Kathleen stood by you and your father all these years while Fiona's been gadding about New York.

> DANNY
>
> Aunt Jenny, I love Kathleen and appreciate what's she's done for me, but Fiona is a part of me I need to understand.

Sean's face is so full of emotion that my heart leaps out to him. His beautiful blue eyes plead with Colleen.

                          DANNY
                       [continued]
             When she goes back to New York, I'm going
             with her.

An anguished voice says, *"Don't go!"*
Sean looks up from his script, startled.
"Uh, that's not the line, Leigh," Colleen says, pointing to the script.
Oops. I've been so caught up in Sean's acting that I haven't
been following along. "Right, sorry," I say. "Where are we?"
"Top of page one hundred and two," Colleen prompts me. *"New
York is . . ."*

                          SINEAD
             New York is so far away, Danny. To Aunt
             Jenny tell him he can't go.

Phew! Nice recovery, if I do say so myself. I hope Roger notices
that this line could use a little doctoring, though. It doesn't even
make sense.
    Roger sighs, shaking his head. He's noticed. Obviously, the young
actress and her director already have an understanding. "Kid," he
says, "don't read the words in brackets. They're screen directions. *'To
Aunt Jenny'* means that Sinead turns to Jenny to deliver the last line."
    "Let's pick it up at Jenny's line," Colleen says quickly, to cover
for my embarrassment.

                          JENNY
             Think about your sister. She depends on you.

                          DANNY
             She's almost fourteen. She can visit me in
             New York.

Almost fourteen? The script very clearly says fifteen in two places, on page thirty-one and on page ninety-seven. Who does he think he is, ad-libbing like that?

> SINEAD
> It won't be the same. I need you here.

The conversation continues between Aunt Jenny and Danny. I follow along, nervously flipping to page 110 every few seconds. That's where I have my next big line. At least, the letters are big. In fact, the line is all in capitals. Sinead must be shouting. Determined to prove to Sean that I can do this, I rehearse the line in my head over and over again.

Finally, they reach page 110 and it's my turn:

> SINEAD
> YOU'RE NOT LISTENING TO ME. YOU *NEVER*
> LISTEN TO ME. I SAID YOU CAN'T LEAVE!

My voice echoes in the trailer. I look up at the others, alarmed. That was more forceful than I intended. Almost hysterical-sounding. Obviously poor Sinead is wound a little tight.

The others are looking at me curiously. Smiling, Sean puts his hand on my shoulder and continues, speaking very gently:

> DANNY
> I do listen to you. But I have to go,
> Sinead, I'm sorry. You'll understand some-
> day.

Hastily checking the script, I notice it does not mention Danny placing his hand on Sinead's shoulder. Now that's a brilliant ad-lib on Sean's part! My performance has inspired him.

We run the scene a few more times, until Colleen's walkie-talkie crackles to life, calling everyone to set. Sean collects his things and thanks us. Then, to my complete shock, he leans over and kisses me on the cheek.

"Leigh," he says, "I appreciate your enthusiasm."

```
A,
He kissed me. ☺
He kissed me. ☺
He kissed me. ☺
He kissed me. ☺
L
```

No need to tell Abby—until she asks—that it wasn't on the lips.

★ ★ ★

I sit in my mother's director's chair, watching her finish her scene. Sean seems to be struggling a bit, and it's no wonder. Mom isn't giving him much to work with. Where's the emotion? The volume? Sean needs that. He plays off it. Since the rehearsal earlier, it's become clear to me where Mom's weakness lies: her acting is too low-key. Too blah. Maybe I'll offer her some pointers over dinner tonight.

"*Cut!*" Roger yells. "We've got that, people, let's move on. Good job, Annika—nice and subtle."

What does Roger know about acting anyway?

"How did the rehearsal go, darling?" Mom asks, as I climb out of her chair.

I shrug. "It was okay." I make a point of sounding bored. "I'd rather be sightseeing."

Since Finian told me about the Blarney Stone, I've realized it's exactly what I need to move things along with Sean. I'm hoping to wear Mom down with constant reminders.

"You're not going sightseeing on your own, so put that thought right out of your mind."

"Which means I'll never go, because you'll never take me."

"Many girls would give their eyeteeth for a chance to hang around a movie set. Who knows, if you pay attention and study hard, you could follow in my footsteps someday."

What's to study, I wonder bitterly. Following in Mom's footsteps isn't rocket science. I could blow off university, marry young, then move away to follow my dream when my kid's only three. But why would I want to?

"Acting is boring," I say. "I'm going to have a normal career, like Dad's."

"Suit yourself." She hands me her script binder and a stack of new pages to insert. "If accounting turns your crank, then go for it. I can't think of anything more mind-numbing myself."

"Dad has a rule about not dissing you," I offer. "He says it's not classy."

That shuts her up. She pulls a compact from the pouch that I've attached to the side of her chair, turns away, and starts powdering her nose.

★ ★ ★

I am sitting on the floor surrounded by new script pages when Colleen approaches. "Just the people I'm looking for," she says, beaming. "I want to offer Leigh the role of Sinead, Sean's sister. If she's interested, that is." Her eyes are twinkling.

Interested in spending day after day working with Sean? Oh, yeah! I must have wowed them at the rehearsal.

Mom says, "I don't think so, Colleen."

"But, Annika, we need her. The girl we cast is out with mono. She's already been in some wide shots and Leigh resembles her."

"Really." My mother looks skeptical.

"You saw her, Annika—the tall one with the shoulder-length brown hair. Fin can give Leigh a trim and she'll pass. We're reducing her lines so that she won't have to speak much."

Okay, so maybe *wowed* was a bit strong, but I can learn. Noticing my mother watching me with an odd expression on her face, I shuffle my papers and try to act cool.

"Does it pay anything, Colleen?" I ask, all businesslike.

"Oh yes. A lot more than your personal assistant wages, I'm betting."

"Right, I'll do it." Visions of new clothes, new makeup, tattoos, and piercings dance in my head, but I know better than to admit to it. Instead, I say, "I'm saving for college."

My mother sniffs. "I thought you said acting was boring," she says.

I can't figure out why she doesn't look happier about this news. "I thought *you* said you'd like me to follow in your footsteps."

"It takes years to learn this craft, Leigh. I meant that you could study drama and try out for school plays. You could make a fool of yourself if you take on too much too soon."

"She'll do fine," Colleen says. "It's just a small role. We're in a bit of a bind because we're scheduled to shoot a scene with Sinead tomorrow."

"Leigh is here on summer holiday, Colleen. She needs to be sightseeing, not spending long days on set." *Excuse me?* "Besides, our father would disapprove."

Well, mine certainly would, but what he doesn't know won't hurt him.

Lowering her voice to a whisper, Colleen says, "Annika, I know you're her mother." My mother gasps and puts her hand over her mouth. "Don't worry, I haven't said anything. But I know you can give Leigh permission."

"She's too young for this life, Colleen."

I get to my feet so that I can look her in the eye. "You weren't much older when *you* started."

She glares at me. "And it's been one long struggle," she says. "You have no idea how hard this job is."

It doesn't seem that hard to me. Maybe she's afraid I'll find out that anyone can do it. Or maybe she's jealous that I'm being given a lucky break.

"Mom, I want to be a veterinarian. Do you know how many years of college you and Dad will be paying for? This will give me a head start."

Ignoring me, Mom turns back to Colleen. "Surely Roger wouldn't hire an inexperienced unknown."

No sooner are the words out of her mouth than Roger appears. "Annika, did Colleen speak to you about giving the kid the role of Sinead?" he asks, looking past me with his bulbous eyes. "I don't have time to recast. The studio is after me to keep the picture on schedule."

Colleen says, "I did ask her Roger, but—"

"—Leigh would be *delighted!*" my mother interrupts smoothly. "Anything to help you, Roger. But I don't want her to be over-worked. She's only fifteen and has no experience memorizing lines."

"I have a photographic memory," I offer helpfully.

"Don't brag, darling," Mom says. "We all know you go to a school for the gifted."

Roger and Colleen laugh and my face flushes. I was just trying to show I could do the job, but it came out sounding conceited.

"I'm sure the kid can do it," Roger says to my mother, as if I'm not even in the room. "And we're reducing the part anyway. We'll only need her for a couple of scenes a week."

"Well, all right," Mom says. "But I have to look out for my little sister, you know."

Colleen and I smother our smiles as Roger turns to leave. Ignoring us, Mom retreats to her trailer with a headache.

★ ★ ★

She's snoring again. I have to remember to use this as ammunition when she's getting on my nerves. It's definitely not something she'd like the tabloids to know: "Annika Anderson Seeks Surgical Solution for Snoring."

Actually, I find the noise oddly comforting tonight as I lie on my lumpy cot, arms crossed behind my head. She's barely said a word to me since agreeing to let me play Sinead in *Danny Boy*. And it's not as if I can sleep anyway. Tomorrow, I'm making my first appearance in front of the camera and I can't stop running through possible scenarios:

Scene 7: Leigh Joins the Cast

Mary and Maude are putting the finishing touches on Leigh's Versace skirt, which has been custom-tailored to her unique BMI. There's a rap on her trailer door.

LEIGH

Come!

ROGER

Hello, darling, I hope you like my old trailer. I've given the painters the color chips you chose and by tomorrow it will scream "Leigh Reid."

LEIGH

No hurry, Roggie. I know this was all very sudden.

                    ROGER
We're just thrilled you accepted the role,
Ms. Reid.

                    LEIGH
Call me Leigh, Rog. Really. It's enough
that you've stopped calling me kid.

                    ROGER
If you insist, Leigh. And I'm sorry
about the kid bit. I didn't realize how
unusually mature you are. Now, I'd like
you to take a look at these new script
pages. Sean was so taken with your
talent during rehearsal yesterday that
he asked us to write additional scenes
for you. It's a lot of dialogue. I hope
you won't find it overwhelming on your
first day.

                    LEIGH
Please, Roger. You're talking to a pro.

Maybe I should offer to meet with those script doctors to share
some of my ideas. What I'm thinking is that Sinead's character
would work far better as Danny's eighteen-year-old girlfriend rather
than his sister. Why waste the chemistry we obviously have? All
that emotion can only improve the movie. But I don't want to look
any more conceited in front of Roger and Colleen right now, so I'll
start by making the best of what I've been given. If I'm good
enough, they'll want to expand my part. That's how this business
works.

Scene 8: Leigh's Big-Screen Debut

*Danny's stepmother, father, and Aunt Jenny have gath-
ered in the O'Leary living room to hear about his first
meeting with Fiona, his long-lost mother. Sinead,
Danny's younger sister, arrives home from school in
time to join them and pours sherry for everyone. This
being a liberal household, she pours one for herself,
too. She glides across the set in her MTV-worthy,
Catholic schoolgirl outfit, hands Danny his sherry,
and joins him on the sofa.*

DANNY

How was school today?

SINEAD

Boring, what else? But let's talk about
your day. You've just met the woman who
gave you life.

DANNY
[speaking softly]

I did.

KATHLEEN

I don't see why you care about Fiona. She
ran off and left you. I'm the one who cried
with you when you fell off your bicycle
and broke your arm.

MR. O'LEARY

Can't you see how this is hurting your
mother?

                    SINEAD
        [her voice shaking with emotion]
Can't you see how this is hurting *Danny?*
He loves us all, Da, but he needs to know
the woman whose blood courses through
his veins. We have to support him. Your
disapproval will tear him apart.

                    DANNY
        [tears streaming down his face]
Sinead, you're the only one who under-
stands me.

                    ROGER
                 [off set]
Cut! Print! [He steps onto the set, his own
eyes glistening.] Ms. Reid—I mean Leigh—
that was riveting, absolutely riveting.

    Mom gives a particularly loud snort in her sleep. Everyone's a
critic.

seven

C ut!" Roger's disembodied voice rises from the darkness beyond the set. "What the hell are you doing?" Sean, Danny's "parents," and I look at each other. One of us is in trouble and I have a feeling it's me. "Are you deaf, kid?"

Yup, it's me. But before he can start in with a lecture, I want to nip this "kid" stuff in the bud. It was annoying enough when I was merely a spectator, but now that I've joined the cast, it's got to go.

"My name is Leigh," I call helpfully toward the directors' chairs grouped around the monitor, where Roger and the producers sit to watch the scene.

"Annika said it was Veronica or Viola or something."

"She calls me Vivien, but it's really Leigh."

"I don't have time to learn a hundred names, kid, I'm a busy man. Let's stick with 'kid.'"

Obviously, there's production-wide conspiracy to prevent me from being treated like an adult. "But how will I know you mean me?"

"Do you see any other kids on this set?"

I consider pointing out that Sean isn't exactly mature, but resist the urge. "No."

"So it should be easy enough."

"But it would be just as easy to call me Leigh. Both words have one syllable."

A low groan ripples across the set and Colleen, who's standing beside the camera, shakes her head warningly.

Roger immediately appears beside her. "Is that an attitude, kid?"

"No." It's a lot harder to have an attitude when I can actually see his face. He's not looking too friendly right now.

"Good, because I don't allow attitude on my set."

I can't see my mother in the gloom, but I can feel her smirking.

Colleen steps to my defense: "She's new to set protocol, Roger."

"Okay," Roger says, "a quick lesson on set protocol for the kid: I am the boss. The boss makes all the rules. And rule number one is that anyone under the age of twenty-one calls me 'sir.' Even Sean, who's twenty-one, calls me 'sir' when he's pissed me off. Right, Sean?"

"Yes sir," Sean says, on cue, looking like he's enjoying the exchange.

"Have I made myself clear, kid?"

"Yes sir." He was so much nicer yesterday during rehearsal when I was doing him a favor. Now that I'm part of the cast, he's treating me like one of his slaves.

"That's better. Now, could you please explain to me what the hell you were doing when we were rolling?"

"Pouring beer. Sir."

Roger taps his script. "It says here that Sinead pours Danny a glass of beer, hands it to him, and sits down. What's with the second glass?"

"I'm pouring one for myself," I explain patiently. Roger, being from L.A., obviously isn't aware of how advanced Irish culture is when it comes to teenagers and alcohol. Even Sean has invited me out for a pint. "You know, to be sociable."

"Really. Does your father encourage you to drink beer at home to be *sociable?*"

The crew chuckles and my face starts to flush. "Well, no, but this is Ireland."

"Children do not drink in Ireland, either."

"But teenagers do."

"Excuse me?"

"Teenagers do, sir, and I'm sixteen."

There's a mumbled protest in the shadows and it's coming from Glazed Poppy lips.

"Kid, do you know where this movie will be airing?"

"In the States, sir?"

"Correct. And legal drinking age there would be?"

"Nineteen, sir."

"In the northern wastelands of Canada, maybe. In our country, it's still twenty-one. Either way, *Sinead* is only fifteen."

"I see your point, sir. Thank you for explaining it to me." Acting is turning out to be a little too similar to school for my liking.

"My pleasure. Shall we resume filming, everyone?"

"You know, Roger," Sean says, "I was thinking that Danny wouldn't likely be drinking beer so early in the day anyway. Why don't we make it a cup of tea?"

Roger stares at Sean for a moment, trying to determine if this is more attitude that must be beaten down. Finally, he turns and nods to the head of the Props Department. There's a flurry of activity and ten minutes later, I'm standing on my mark in front of a pot of tea and a china cup on a saucer.

"Roll camera," Roger says.

The camera assistant shoves a slate in front of my face. "Scene seventy-two, take two," she says, smacking the sticks of the slate together under my nose.

"Action!" Roger calls, now back in his chair near the monitors.

The loud smack of the slate has rattled my nerves but I rise to the occasion, pouring the tea into the cup. I try putting myself into the mind-set of Sinead, who's just home from school, but my thoughts keep wandering. I can't help thinking about the way Sean jumped in to protect me from the big bad director. He's my knight in shining armor! Of course, he might actually believe that Danny would be more likely to drink tea than beer in this scene, but I prefer to think that we have a new understanding. Because I'm working with him, he's seeing me differently—more like an equal. Maybe he's even starting to fall for me. After all, he did kiss me the other day and if Colleen hadn't been there, it might have been a real kiss.

The thought gives me such a thrill that my hand starts shaking as I pick up the tea and walk toward Sean. The delicate cup rattles in the saucer and the more aware of it I become, the louder the clattering grows. I try to anchor the cup in the saucer with my other hand before the "boom" man, who's recording the sound on set, catches on. Just two more steps to go and—

"Cut! I hear a noise, people." Roger has an animated conversation with the boom man before saying, "Props, dump the cup and saucer. We need a mug out here." The props man runs back to the truck and a few minutes later we start again.

"Scene seventy-two, take three."

This time my hand is already shaking as I pour the tea and I accidentally fill the mug until it slops over the brim. Afraid of dribbling all over the set, I walk with extra care across what now seems like a vast expanse of living room. Before I'm even halfway there, Roger says *cut*.

"It's only a two-hour movie, kid. Were you planning on delivering that tea sometime before we wrap? Or wait, maybe the script says, 'Sinead minces toward Danny at a snail's pace.'" He pretends to consult the script. "Nope, it doesn't."

There's no need for sarcasm, but I am not in a position to protest. "Sorry, sir, I'll pick up the pace."

"Scene seventy-two, take four."

I pour the tea quickly, filling the mug only halfway, and begin the trek across the set. This time I am so intent on speed that I forget to glance down and stumble over some wires. The tea splatters onto a white linen cloth that's draped over a coffee table.

"Cut! Props?" The props man takes a moment to glare at me before running back to his truck to get another tablecloth.

"Scene seventy-two, take five."

By some miracle, I manage to deliver the tea to Sean in a quiet, timely manner. I perch on the arm of his chair as he delivers his lines, heaving a sigh of relief. Now I can relax and enjoy this magic moment, as Sean and I are filmed together for the first time. Someday, Abby will sit in a darkened multiplex, watching Sean and me on the big screen, and see how it all started. By that time, we'll probably be engaged.

"Kid?" Roger's voice is unnaturally calm as he steps onto the set again. "Have you read this scene?"

"Yes, at least ten times. I mean, at least ten times, sir." Probably more like fifty, but no need to look too keen.

"Then maybe you'll recall that the script says 'Sinead pours the drink, delivers it to Danny, and then *sits on the sofa between her parents.*' It does not say 'Sinead drapes herself over the arm of Danny's chair and gazes at him like a devoted basset hound.' Paramount Studios has paid good money for this script to be shot the way it is written. If it's good enough for them, it's good enough for you."

The other actors are sniggering and I can't really blame them. Still, I do not look like a basset hound and I can't believe my mother is just sitting there letting him insult me like that. But then, she let him call her an iguana once and that's definitely worse than a hound.

"Sorry," I repeat.

"Let's try it again, shall we? And this time, please join the rest of us in following the script."

The camera assistant claps the slate half-heartedly. "Scene seventy-two, take six."

I really focus this time and manage to pour the tea into the mug, deliver it to Sean, and take my place on the sofa without incident. It's simple, really. Why couldn't I get it right the first time? Obviously I just needed a few takes to get a feel for acting. Now that I've mastered it, I'm free to study the others until the scene ends. If only this costume were more comfortable. Sinead's school outfit consists of a baggy, shin-length, plaid wool jumper and a mustard-colored school sweater. Under the bright lights, the wool is hot and unbelievably itchy.

"Cut, cut, cut!" I look around hopefully at the others. Since my job is done, obviously someone else is going to suffer Roger's wrath this time. "What's your name, again, kid? Vanessa? Verna?"

"Vivien, sir. Vivien Leigh—from *Gone with the Wind,* you know. I go by Leigh."

Roger scowls. "I don't care if you're named after Marilyn Bloody Monroe. I asked you to take over this role to *save* time and money, not to *lose* it."

"I don't get it. I was sitting here like you said, sir."

"That's it exactly: I said 'sit,' not squirm like you're dangling over an open flame. You're disrupting the entire shot!"

Working himself into a rant, Roger starts listing every mistake I've made while I stare at the floor, fighting back tears. Finally, my mother gets out of her chair and walks over to him. It's about time she took action. She should tower over the vicious little troll and tell him he can't talk to me like this. No one messes with the daughter— er, make that sister—of Annika Anderson. You go, Mom!

"Roger," she says, touching his arm gently to calm him down, "yelling isn't going to accomplish anything." I was hoping for a stronger attack, but it's better than nothing. "You're going to have to accept that you made a serious mistake in casting someone with no acting experience and choose someone else."

What?

"It's not like I wanted to cast her," he says. "I had no choice.

We're running out of time and money and I don't have the luxury of shuffling scenes around until we find a new Sinead." He turns to me. "For God's sake, Veronica, this is simple stuff. You don't even have a line."

I whisper, so that my voice won't quaver. "It's Leigh."

"Don't you dare start crying, young lady. We're paying you to do a job here—a job you said you wanted yesterday. So start concentrating and get it right."

"Roger, she isn't cut out for acting," Annika says. "And now she's so flustered she'll never get it right. Find someone else to take over."

How dare she say I'll *never* get it right just because I've blown it six times? Yesterday, she blew twelve takes on something almost as simple and she's had twenty-five years of experience. She doesn't know what I can do. Maybe Veronica, Vanessa, and Viola give up, but Leigh Reid does not. Leigh Reid has stood up to bullies before—okay, one bully in junior high—and she will do it again. Leigh Reid does not run away.

I get off the couch and take a couple of determined steps toward Roger. "Please don't find someone else, sir. I can do this and I promise I will get it right."

```
Abs,
Actin iz a lot harder
thN it LXkz. 1st dA
wz a disaster. d troll
wntd 2 kill me & my
mum wntz me 2 quit,
which I won't. d onlE
gud tng dat hapnd wz
dat Sean punched me n
d arm 18r & sed 'don't
```

```
GIU uP kid.'
Ireland sux.
L
```

★   ★   ★

"How about another helping, young wan?" Mrs. O'Reilly says, carrying the pot of stew to the table. Although I've already eaten two servings, I nod eagerly. I was too nervous to eat all day and besides, this is the best stew I've ever eaten. Pushing my bowl toward Mrs. O'Reilly, I tell her so. "Of course," she says, in a matter-of-fact voice. "I make the best mutton stew in the county. Everyone knows that." She pats her curlers with obvious pride.

"Mutton? What's mutton?"

"Lord, what do yez eat in that godforsaken country o' yours? Mutton is sheep."

"Sheep! But they're so cute!"

"And tasty, too."

It occurs to me that I haven't seen Skip for a couple of days. If he doesn't appear by breakfast, I'm becoming a vegetarian just in case he arrives on my plate. Shoving my bowl in front of Annika, I say, "Try some. I haven't poisoned it—although I should."

"Look," she says, picking at her plate of raw vegetables, "I've told you a million times that I was just trying to help. Acting is an emotionally charged career and I don't think you have the right personality for it. I was trying to spare you the misery."

"And I've told you a million times that I want to be a vet, not an actor. But I signed on to play Sinead and I am not a quitter. Dad makes me follow through on whatever I promise to do." Which is true, but that wouldn't stop me from quitting now if it weren't for Sean—and the satisfaction of annoying her.

"Then you'd better learn to deal with tough directors because it's part of the package." She reaches for her cigarettes and pushes her chair back from the table. Wrapping a scarf around her hair, she steps out into the drizzly night and closes the door so firmly behind her that it would be called slamming if I did it.

"She's the worst mother on the planet," I point out to Mrs. O'Reilly, in case she hasn't noticed this herself.

"That she's not, gersha. I've seen many worse." She ladles custard over fresh raspberries and hands me a bowl. She prepares another bowl for herself and takes my mother's place at the table, tugging at the edges of her gaping bathrobe. "Now don't pay yer woman no mind. She'll come around."

Mrs. O'Reilly is so sympathetic all of sudden that I wonder if she's been hitting the sauce. "I don't care what Annika thinks anyway," I say, which is almost true. I wouldn't care at all if I were at home, but since I'm stuck with her twenty-four/seven at the moment, I do care a little.

"Your ma's had a desperate time of it lately, so she told me. She's getting on in years and you Americans give hard neck to anyone over thirty." Mrs. O'Reilly has clearly fallen for Annika's whole "poor aging me" shtick. "And now, with all she's got to worry about, suddenly she has to be yer mam as well."

"Yeah, well, she's had plenty of time to work up to it."

"Seeing her babby a grown up young lady hasn't helped, I'm sure. Now you're becoming an actress, too. You know yer ma struggled for donkey's years before landing a wee part in a flick and here you are, getting handed a role just for being in the right place at the right time."

"So? Any normal mother would be happy for me. It's not like I'm trying to steal the spotlight from her. I'm not even interested in acting. Besides, I never wanted to spend the summer with her in the first place. My father made me. And now that I'm here, she won't even let me see Ireland."

"You said you hated this—what was it—this 'moldy, sheep-infested country.'"

"I said 'soggy,' but it's starting to grow on me." And it is, too. Now that I'm getting used to how quiet Bray is, I like being in the country. I've started exploring the lanes around the cottage when the sun shines and I can't help admiring the green hills. I've even discovered a spot on a deserted stretch of beach that's perfect for hiding out with a book. "But I want to see more than Bray before I go home. Do you think Blarney Castle is worth a visit, Mrs. O?"

"Looking for the gift of the gab, are ye?" She gives me a knowing look. "I made the trip to Blarney myself when I was your age."

"So that you could charm Mr. O'Reilly?" It's hard to imagine Mrs. O'Reilly trying to attract anyone, let alone weather-beaten old Mr. O'Reilly, but stranger things have happened.

"Cop on to yourself! Yer man was lucky to get me. I'm thinking of me first love, Thomas Connery." She pats her curlers again and smiles as she tells me her story.

Thomas Connery was a handsome young man from Scotland who came to work on his uncle's sheep farm in Ireland one summer when he was fifteen. Within days of his arrival, the local girls were clamoring to ride around on the back of his motorcycle. Thomas already had the god-given gift of the gab, but Mrs. O was always at a loss for words when he was around, so she and her sister Sheena hitchhiked to Blarney to kiss the famous stone. That evening, when the girls arrived back in Bray, she began to dazzle Thomas with her newfound charm. All at once it seemed they had everything in common. They rode on his motorcycle to Malone's Cliff, where they watched the sun set and talked as though there weren't enough hours left in their lives to tell each other all that they had to say.

"And you think it was the Blarney stone that gave you these magical powers?" I ask, skeptically.

Mrs. O shovels an enormous spoonful of custard into her mouth. "Think what you will, young wan. All I'm saying is that Thomas Connery and I were inseparable for the rest of that sweet summer."

"What happened to Thomas after that?"

"He moved to England to become an actor."

"Really?" I lean forward in my seat. "Did he succeed?"

"You could say that." She stands to collect our empty bowls. "Ever heard of Agent Double-oh-seven?"

"James Bond? I don't remember a Bond named Thomas Connery."

As my mother steps back into the kitchen, Mrs. O leans over and whispers in my ear: "His middle name was Sean."

"No way!"

Mrs. O'Reilly puts a forefinger to her mouth to silence me and winks.

"What's going on?" my mother asks.

In response, Mrs. O begins to warble an Irish folk song about lost love. She has a nice singing voice that makes her sound younger. If it weren't for the curlers and bathrobe, I could almost imagine her with Sean Connery.

Almost, but not quite.

eight

Unlike most of the students in my school, I am not a genius. I just have a good memory. Dad says there's no such thing as a photographic memory, but even he admits mine is good—so good that Abby accuses me of breezing through most of my subjects, which isn't entirely true. There are plenty of things I have to work at, like English; finding themes, symbolism, and metaphors takes a lot more than a good memory. Dad wishes I'd work harder at school. He's afraid I'll develop poor study habits because I rely on my memory too much. "One day it will fade," he says, "and then where will you be?" I've already noticed that it's not as sharp as it used to be. I think it's because my mind is too busy and cluttered. Dad helpfully points out that it was never too busy or cluttered before I got interested in boys. Whatever. I just hope it's still working for me by the time I get into college, where I'll really need it.

As with English, acting is not something you can just memorize and call up when you need it. At least, if there's formula, I don't know what it is and my mother isn't about to share it. If I were at home, I'd check some books on drama out of the library. Since I'm not, I guess I'll have to learn by trial and error. I'm involved in three different scenes today, so I hope there's a lot less error than yesterday.

When Roger sees me cowering on the edges of the set for the O'Learys' living room, he frowns. The friendliness he showed during the rehearsal two days ago has not reappeared. Not that I care what he thinks. He can ignore me, for all I care. I just don't want him to fire me. It's not as if I could quietly leave the production in disgrace, like any other cast member would. I'm practically chained to my mother's director's chair; I won't be going anywhere for weeks.

Strangely enough, I don't even want to go anywhere now. I want to stay here until Sean realizes we're meant to be together—for life. Then it will be safe to go back to the States and wait until he gets his immigration papers lined up. At worst, we could keep up a long distance romance until I finish high school and then I'll follow him to L.A. As it happens, the University of California has a veterinary medicine program. It's amazing what a simple Internet search turns up.

But first things first. Before I let him talk me into leaving Seattle for him, I have to get him to stop laughing his "arse" off every time he sees me. As hard as I try, I can't figure out how to impress him—to take me seriously. Reciting the periodic table of the elements might work on a nerd like Glen Myers, but I know that it would only earn me more ridicule from Sean. Instead, I have to figure out how to play a fifteen-year-old Irish girl whose brother is leaving, when I don't even have a brother. Why did I ever think taking this part was a good idea?

"We need Sinead in the background," Roger calls. When I step onto the set, he adds, "Keep it simple today, will you, kid? Just do what the script says for a change."

"Fine." I look at Sean, who's leaning against the set's doorway, watching me.

"Pardon me?" Roger asks, wearing the same "don't talk back to me" expression I see on my father all the time.

"I said, fine, *sir.*"

"Right, then. As you know, we don't always shoot scenes in the order of the story. This scene takes place just before the one we shot yesterday. Sean, Danny will be watching TV, flipping channels when Kathleen comes into the room. You're depressed. You're studying American television and wondering if a working-class Irish boy can ever fit in there, if you can be cool enough for New York. Viola, Sinead's sitting at the dining room table doing her homework. You should know all about that, being a *gifted* student."

It's funny how Roger can remember that detail, but my name is too much for him.

Sean laughs and slaps me on the shoulder as I cross in front of him to sit down at the table. "Shut up," I say. Forget about impressing him.

Opening the history textbook in front of me, I pick up a pen and pretend to take notes.

"And . . . rolling," Roger calls. Danny walks across the living room, throws himself into an armchair, and turns on the television with the remote control. He begins flicking through station after station, leaning forward in his seat when he picks up MTV. "*Cut!* That's good. Let's do it again, only slow down the station changes, Sean, and no drooling when you get to MTV. You're wondering how true to American life those videos are."

We do the scene a few times before Roger is satisfied. I expect some harsh words about the way I hold my pen, but amazingly, he has no complaints at all. Things are looking up.

When I stand to leave the table, Sean comes over. "Maybe we'll make an actress out of you yet," he says, reaching around me for the notebook on the table. I try to grab it out of his hand, but it's too late. "Why, look at this . . . Along with some key facts on the Boer War, your notes say 'LR loves DB.' In a huge heart, no less. Who's DB? The eejit of a boyfriend who sacked you?"

I jump for the notebook, which he's holding out of reach above his head and gasp, "None of your business!"

"Aha! DB could be *Danny Boy*."

"If you *must* know," I say, my face burning, "it stands for Devin Bainbridge, a boy in my class."

"At the school for brainiacs? Bet he's a molly."

"He is not a molly! Devin is talented and smart—and really nice."

"Sounds like a wanker to me. You're welcome to him if that's your type." He swaggers off with a look of mock disgust.

★　★　★

Mom is already on set, in full makeup, although her scene won't come up for a couple of hours. I suppose she was hoping to see me go down in flames. Well, she'll be disappointed today. I'm catching on to this whole Sinead thing.

Without waiting to be asked, I get her a cappuccino from craft services. Then I tell her that Sean and Colleen have gone outside for a smoke—that she could catch up with them if she hurries. She eyes me suspiciously, sensing I have an agenda. And she's right: I'm softening her up with nicotine and caffeine before chatting to her about our weekend plans.

When she returns, I hand her a perfectly organized script binder and try my luck. "Tomorrow's Saturday, Annika. How about doing some sightseeing?"

"Not this again."

"Come on, I can't go home without experiencing some Irish culture. Let's go to Blarney Castle."

"Darling, it's too far. And I'm not about to drive a rental car on the wrong side of the road. That wouldn't be good for either of us, believe me."

Colleen, who has followed Mom back to set after their smoke, says, "You don't need to drive, Annika. We'll pay your driver to take you around on the weekend if you like. He can take you to Blarney Castle."

"I'm too tired," Mom snaps. "I can't chase a teenager around after such a grueling week." She settles into her chair with the cappuccino, looking disgruntled.

"I'm free tomorrow. Why don't I come along with you and play tour guide? Leigh and I can run around and you can rest in the car. Later, we'll get manicures and have dinner."

Mom loves getting her nails done and Colleen knows it. I can see who the genius is on this set. Mom shrugs and nods, prompting Sean, who is hovering nearby, to ask, "How about letting me join the tour, Annie?"

"Forget it, boyo," Colleen jumps in, before my mother can say anything. "It's a civilized outing. Girls only."

I glare at Colleen and she meets my eyes coolly.

★   ★   ★

My second scene calls for Sinead to look out the window, turn to Kathleen, her mother, and say three words: **"Ma, Danny's home."** It's not much, but I'm nervous because I have to say it with an Irish accent. The dialogue coach spent about five minutes with me this morning before my mother called him away, demanding help with her own lines. I asked every Irish crew member to deliver the line for me, but that only confused matters since no two accents are alike in this country. In the end, I settled on a mixture of Colleen and Sean and I think it sounds pretty authentic.

"Rolling," Roger calls.

I look out the set window into the wall beyond and turn.

SINEAD

    Ma, Danny's home.

Danny opens the door and steps onto the set. Flawless! Even my accent was "spot on," as Fin would say.

"Cut! Kid, you turned so fast all I saw was a wall of hair. Slow it down. And . . . rolling."

SINEAD

Ma, Danny's home.

"Cut! What was that, slow motion? Just a natural turn, kid."

SINEAD

Ma, Danny's home.

"Cut! You're tossing your hair. It's not a damn shampoo commercial. Careful, or I'll have Finian put it in pigtails."

That threat makes me focus doubly hard. Not too fast, not too slow, natural turn. I can do this. What I can't do is look at Sean, who's been walking in the door after my line and out again when I blow the take.

SINEAD

Ma, Danny's home.

"Cut. Better. You've got the turn, but the tone is off. Warm it up a little. You're happy he's home. You know he won't be around much longer."

SINEAD

Ma, Danny's home.

"Cut. Not bad, but warmer still."

SINEAD

Ma, Danny's home—*at last.*

"Cut. What was that?"

"I, uh, just, ad-libbed . . ."

Roger steps over to me. "Do not—I repeat—*do not* ad-lib on my set."

"I just thought it would sound like she's already missing him."

"The only person who thinks on this set is me," he shouts. "What do they teach you at that school for the gifted, anyway? Now, listen to me carefully: Danny is getting home after a *day's work,* not an expedition to Nepal."

"Right, sorry."

"You should be." His voice is level again, but as sharp as broken glass. "On *my* set, children are meant to be seen and not heard. Especially when their accents say Liverpool rather than Dublin. Colleen, get the dialogue coach out here."

My mother is not gloating exactly, but there's a little pucker around her mouth that suggests she's enjoying my disgrace. I suppose it's just as well that she isn't more sympathetic; sympathy would probably make me cry. Colleen beckons me, but I pretend I don't see her, shrinking as low as I can behind some props.

Finally the dialogue coach arrives to remove Liverpool from my three-word line. Meanwhile, Roger shares his disappointment with my mother, loud enough that I can hear. "Working with the kid is really slowing us down," he says.

"She has no training or experience, Roger. As I said yesterday, you should find someone else."

"I don't have time to find someone else."

"In the long run, it will save time."

"Maybe it would. I just thought she'd have your talent, you know?"

"Oh Roger, that's lovely of you to say. Thank you, darling."

My mother is purring, her hand on Roger's scrawny arm. I feel like throwing up. I can't possibly be that bad. But if I am, at least there's nowhere to go but up.

"I'm going to need physio for my arm, all that door-opening and closing," Sean jokes as I walk onto the set. I try to smile, knowing he's making an effort to cheer me up, but it's no use. "Don't look so blue," he continues, "I'll tell you something that'll perk you up: on day one of *Danny Boy,* Roger said my Irish accent was crap."

"But you're Irish!"

"According to Roger, my accent was still wrong for Danny. Said I sounded like bloody bogger."

"That's *terrible.* Uh, what's a bogger?"

"A country bumpkin. Born and raised twenty miles from Dublin center and I'm spending hours with his bloody dialogue coach. Unbelievable."

Feeling better in spite of myself, I say, "This is harder than I expected."

"Good actors make it look easy, but there's a lot of work involved. Haven't you noticed how Annika goes back to her trailer for some quiet time before each of her scenes?"

"I thought she was napping. She is getting on in years."

Sean ignores this dig. "She's preparing. Acting isn't like school and memorizing the lines won't get you an A. You've got to invest a bit of yourself in them."

"But I feel lame investing myself."

"At the beginning, everyone is hyperaware. It's like you're thinking, *what right do I have to be playing Sinead—this bratty baby sister of a total wanker?* Eventually you will relax and start thinking like Sinead."

"But how? How do I start to think like a character from a script?"

"Some people make up an entire background for their character. For example, I imagine what sports Danny would play, what music he'd like. I even decided that his favorite dish is bangers and mash."

"I could do that for Sinead."

"Start by asking yourself, *What would Sinead do in this situation?*

Like she's a real person. Don't say it out loud though, or everyone will think you're off your nut."

Roger bellows, "Hello, I am not paying you two to gab all day. Let's take it from the top."

This time I nail it in two takes. There's just enough time between them for Sean to make a show of massaging his arm.

Roger is finally happy, although he says I sound like a Dubliner who went to a snooty Liverpool boarding school. He's almost smiling when he says it, so I guess I did okay.

★   ★   ★

By the time my third scene comes up, I'm totally wiped out. No wonder Mom complains so much. It's way more stressful than it looks being in front of the camera—especially when you're as lousy as I am. And now that I'm trying to create a history for Sinead, I've got even more of a challenge on my hands.

I didn't get the "quiet time" in Mom's trailer that I needed over lunch because the drivers needed to move the trucks to a new location. We're shooting at the Thirsty Leprechaun, a pub that will double as the O'Learys' local bar, Fibber McGee's.

In the scene, Fiona has been invited to join the family for a beer. Sinead and Kathleen are meeting her for the first time. As Fiona is introduced, Sinead says, "So you're Danny's birth mother."

Not only do I have to string five words together with an Irish accent, it's my first scene with Annika and I'm more nervous than I am when I have to write a big exam. At least then I know that only my teacher, Dad, and I need to know how I've done. Here, there's a big audience and Mom is front and center hoping I'll screw up. It's not a good feeling. And it's not fair, either. When I watch her do a scene, I *pray* that she won't screw up. True, I'm less interested in her doing well than in her not embarrassing me, but I'd settle for that in exchange.

The pub is already filled with nearly twenty extras as we take our seats around a low wooden table that is covered in shiny pressed copper. Taking my place beside my mother, I see a familiar face lined up at the bar. The man shoots me a toothless grin and tips his ratty old cap.

"What's Mr. O'Reilly doing here?" I ask my mother.

"It's his local and he refused to leave when the pub closed down for the film. I managed to convince Casting to put him in the scene. You know how grumpy Mrs. O'Reilly gets when he's under-foot all day."

The props guy delivers pint glasses of dark, frothy beer to Annika, Sean, and the actors playing Kathleen and Mr. O'Leary. He slides a glass of soda in front of me. An insult! Sinead has been coming to Fibber Mcgee's with her family every Sunday afternoon since she was a baby—at least according to the back story I've been creating.

"The O'Learys would let Sinead have real beer," I tell the props guy, sliding the soda aside and plucking a beer off his tray.

He snatches the beer out of my hand and reinstates the soda. "Have you lost your mind?"

"What did I tell ya?" Sean asks, in a loud whisper. "They think you're off your nut already. Here, have some of mine." He shoots the glass across the table to me.

Mom reaches out to intercept the glass but I am too fast for her. Grabbing it, I take a big swig—and almost gag. It's not real beer at all, but very strong tea at room temperature topped with something thick and foamy.

"Augh, that's gross." I slide the glass back to Sean, wincing.

"*Now* look what you've done," my mother says to Sean, taking a bar napkin and leaning over to wipe my mouth. When I lean backward to escape her, she grabs my chin and pats my upper lip with the napkin. "Keep still," she hisses as I resist, "you're a mess."

"Frothing like a mad dog," Sean says. He looks pleased with himself.

"It's not funny," my mother and I say together, causing Sean and both "O'Learys" to laugh even harder.

Roger breaks up the party. "Look, you're already arguing like a real family, you fools. Remember, most of you are meeting Fiona for the first time. And except for Danny, you're all very suspicious of her intentions. She's reappeared after seventeen years and you figure she's trying to lure Danny away from you. Okay . . . rolling."

                    MR. O'LEARY
        Fiona, lovely to see you again. This is my
        wife, Kathleen.

                     KATHLEEN
        It's nice to finally meet you, Fiona.

                      FIONA
        Nice to meet you, too, Kathleen. You've
        done a wonderful job raising Danny. You
        must be very proud of him.

                     KATHLEEN
        Oh, we couldn't be prouder. And also of our
        daughter, Sinead, here.

                      FIONA
        Hello, Sinead.

Maybe it's my imagination, but my mother appears to be smirking. Or maybe the fake beer didn't agree with me. At any rate, something seems to be bubbling into my throat, making it hard to breathe.

                          SINEAD
          So...You're Danny's birth mother. You've
          got some nerve coming back here after you
          abandoned him.

There's silence around the table as everyone waits for Roger to
yell *cut*. When he doesn't, Sean begins improvising.

                          DANNY
          Steady on, Sinead. You don't know what
          you're talking about.

                          SINEAD
          Sure I do. She thinks she can just waltz in
          here and make up for all those years in a
          few weeks.

                          DANNY
          Nobody's waltzing, Sinead. But I believe
          in second chances. Don't you?

                          SINEAD
          No! *I'd* throw her out of here on her bony
          arse.

Everyone starts laughing and Roger yells "Cut!" at last. "Take a
break, everyone. Regroup in five." I slide out of the seat and try to
duck behind Sean. "Not so fast, Verna," Roger says. "What did I say
about ad-libbing?"

"Never on *your* set." I let the name slide. Something tells me this
wouldn't be the best time to correct him.

"Right. And . . . ?"

"And no one thinks but you, sir."

"Right again. But in this case, you were *feeling,* and that's another thing entirely." His eyes are enormous behind his dark, rectangular glasses but he doesn't look angry. "As Sinead, how did you feel about meeting Fiona?" he demands.

I think about this for a moment. "Pissed off."

"Bingo. That's exactly how you were supposed to feel. But you still don't get to make up your own lines. Who's set is it?"

"Yours."

"Next take, *feel* the same way, but channel the emotion into the words you're given. And keep the scowling to a minimum, will you? It's a drama, not a farce."

My mother is standing at the bar with Mr. O'Reilly. As our eyes meet, she accepts the cigarette he offers and allows him to light it for her. Exhaling slowly, she continues to watch me through the cloud of smoke.

★   ★   ★

The teakettle is screaming on the burner when we arrive back at the cottage. Because she's now the wife of a film star, perhaps, Mrs. O'Reilly has actually changed into a flowered housedress and brown lace-up shoes. As she turns to the stove, the dress flares slightly, revealing knee-high nylons.

Each night as we've pulled in, Mrs. O'Reilly has been standing by the stove, the kettle boiling. The windows aren't foggy, so it's not like she's had it simmering for hours. Somehow she's known exactly when to turn on the burner. Tonight I can't help but ask, "How do you know when we'll be home?"

"Leprechauns," she answers. She pours water into the pot and shakes chocolate cream biscuits from a package onto a chipped china plate.

"No, really," I say.

"I always know when someone needs a cuppa," she says. "Sit down and I'll bring you one."

There doesn't seem much point in arguing, so I add milk and sugar to the cup she pours me. After all, I drank every drop when Sean served it to me and I didn't mind it. It makes me feel more Irish. Sinead probably drinks a lot of tea. And chocolate cream biscuits happen to be her favorite.

My mother sits down opposite me and stirs her own tea. Breaking a microscopic corner off a cookie, she asks, "So what was that about this afternoon?"

"What do you mean?" I pop an entire cookie into my mouth.

"The ad-libbing in the first take of the pub scene. What got into you?"

"I was just pissed about your wiping my face in front of everyone. I'm not three years old." I spray cookie crumbs onto the table.

"Angry. 'Pissed' is vulgar. And so is talking with your mouth full."

Sometimes the best response is no response at all, so I turn my attention to licking the cream filling out of my second cookie.

"You can't play out your personal dramas when the camera is rolling," she continues.

"But I can use my feelings. Roger said so. Besides, I see Sinead O'Leary as an angry young woman."

She changes direction. "I'm not sure acting is good for you. You seem upset."

"I'm fine. You're the one who needs to lighten up."

Mrs. O'Reilly, sitting on an old wooden chair in the corner, mutters, "Mothers and daughters . . . it's one ruction after another."

Pushing back her chair, Mom walks over to Mrs. O'Reilly, who silently holds out the tin of hand-rolled cigarettes. Mom opens the tin and selects one before turning to pick up the telephone receiver from the counter. She returns to the table and pushes the buttons carefully with her long nails.

"Hello, Dennis," she says, "someone needs to talk to you."

"I do *not* need to talk to him." My voice echoes in the tiny kitchen. She hands me the phone anyway. Sighing, I say, "Hi, Dad."

"Sweetie! I've called you half a dozen times. I was worried you were never going to get over being mad at me."

"I sent you text messages."

"It's not the same. Besides, I can't understand half of what you write. Your grandmother seems to be better at deciphering that code."

"How is Gran?"

"Fine, but Millie's driving her crazy. I brought the dog home for the weekend."

"Can you put her on?" There's a shuffling sound, followed by an urgent repetition of *"Speak, speak."* I can picture Millie going through her whole repertoire of tricks, trying to hit the right one. Finally, she gives a big woof. "Thanks, Dad," I say, "give her a treat for me."

"So, how is it going over there?"

"Fine." Like I am going to say more with Annika staring at me. Not blinking. Roger is right about the iguana comparison.

"Are you getting along with your mother?"

"Not exactly."

"Is she sitting right there?"

"Yeah."

"Well, have patience, Leigh. It's only a few more weeks."

"I'm trying. Well, I'd better go, Dad."

"Already?"

Mom reaches out for the phone with a lizardlike lunge. "Not so fast." To Dad she says, "Your daughter neglected to mention that she's taken a role in my movie. Yes, I know, I know. I tried to discourage her, but she insisted. She's very stubborn. No, that doesn't come from my side of the family! You should be concerned, she seems very . . . *emotional.* Maybe you should tell her to give up the part since she won't listen to me." She hands the phone back to me.

"Forget to tell me something?" he asks.

"Well, it's a very small part, Dad, hardly worth mentioning." I give my mother a defiant look. "You wanted me to spend time with Annika and believe me, I spend a lot of time with her."

"*Annika?*"

"Yeah, that's what she wants me to call her." Now it's Mom's turn to glare. "I even have to share a room with her, if you can believe it." Aware of Mrs. O'Reilly's eyes upon me, I add, "It's a nice room, though."

"Leigh, you know how I feel about acting—particularly for children."

"I'm not a child! Anyway, it's not a career choice, Dad. The director asked me to fill in and they're paying me. I'm saving for college."

Mom rolls her eyes at Mrs. O'Reilly, who gets off her chair and opens the cupboard door. She takes down a bottle of whiskey and sets two glasses on the counter. After pouring an inch of liquor into each glass, she hands one to my mother.

"You won't be skipping college to try your luck in Hollywood, so don't get any big ideas," he says.

"Dad. I still want to be a vet. I'm not going to settle for *acting* like one."

"Well, all right. I will be supervising how you use that money. You're not blowing it all on purple nail polish."

"As if. Annika already made me open up a bank account. My checks are directly deposited and she put a limit on how much I can withdraw."

"I'm glad to hear it."

"Besides, purple nail polish is so last month, Dad. Try to keep up, will you? Look, see you in three weeks."

"Call me once a week. And listen, let's not say anything to Grandma just yet about the acting, okay?"

It's nice to see his performance turning around after such a long dip. I may not need to fire him after all.

nine

A warm loaf of Mrs. O'Reilly's dense, chewy soda bread is sitting on the counter when I step into the kitchen on Saturday morning. Beside it is a note impaled on a bread knife:

> Young wan,
> Eat—you'll need your energy today.
> May the Blarney Stone work its magic on you, too.
> > Yours truly,
> > O'Reilly. Mary O'Reilly.

The reference to James Bond makes me smile. Who'd have guessed that Mrs. O has been hiding a sense of humor under that bathrobe all this time? Not that I need any encouragement to eat her soda bread, mind you. So far, it's my favorite Irish food.

Lucky, our driver, arrives between Annika's sixth and seventh wardrobe change and sits smoking in the idling Audi. Since Goldilocks is having trouble finding something "just right" for Blarney, I decide to use the time to do some character research. Leaning on the car, I say, "Howya, Lucky!" in Sinead's best Dublin accent.

Eying me suspiciously, he growls, "Where's yer mam? I've been waiting for ages already."

"It's been a long week," I say. "Yer woman was wrecked this morning—had a devil of a time gettin' her outta bed. How about giving me a driving lesson while we're waiting?"

Lucky's eyebrows knit together in a frown. "I am in me wick."

I have no idea what he means, but since he isn't making any move to surrender the wheel, I offer, "I'm nearly sixteen."

"What do ye take me fer, a muppet?"

I try again, switching back to my Washington-born-and-bred accent. "It's research, Lucky. Sinead O'Leary spends her summers at her grandparents' farm; she was driving a tractor by the time she was twelve."

"Who the hell is Sinead O'Leary?"

"My character." He looks at me blankly. "In *Danny Boy?*" Still nothing. Before I can launch into a full explanation, a shriek makes me jump away from the car.

"Vivien!" My mother clicks down the path in a blue-and-pink sundress and matching designer sandals. As usual, I marvel at her ability to maneuver over cobblestones in high heels. Annika claims she was born in stilettos, which would explain why Grandma Anderson is such a mean old hag. "What in God's name are you wearing?"

"A jumper." Duh. I slide quickly into the backseat.

"Oh no, you don't," she says, standing at the car door with her hands on her hips. "You are not wearing that ridiculous school pinafore all day. I can't believe Maude let you take it home."

"She said it was fine." Or at least she would have if she'd been in the wardrobe trailer when I stopped by to borrow it for the weekend. "I need to get used to the itchy wool." Not entirely a lie, although the cycling shorts I'm wearing underneath are solving the problem nicely. "Come on, Mom. I'm playing an Irish Catholic schoolgirl. I just want to know what it feels like to be seen that way."

"No Irish girl would be caught dead in her uniform on the

weekend, but if you want to embarrass yourself, who am I to stand in your way?"

She climbs in beside me and Lucky pulls away from the cottage so fast that we're thrown back in our seats. Grassy meadows, ancient stone walls and herds of sheep whiz past at an alarming rate as we speed toward Colleen's cottage. She's already outside waiting when we lurch to a stop. "Howya, Lucky," she says, climbing into the front seat.

"Rough as a bear's arse," he says. "Could have had an extra hour's kip with all the foosterin' these two did this morning." He jerks his thumb in our direction.

She turns to grin at us. "Ah, but it's a grand morning for an outing, isn't it?" I nod eagerly as Colleen's eyes sweep over my outfit. She doesn't say a word.

Lucky slams the car into drive and we're off again, rocketing past sea and field and castle ruins. A dizzying three hours later, we arrive in Blarney, where the car screeches to a halt in front of the Woolen Mills, narrowly missing an elderly couple wearing matching Tilley hats and yellow windbreakers.

"Alright, folks?" Lucky calls, leaping out and tipping his crumpled hat at them. He opens the back door for my mother, while Colleen and I scramble out, eager to have our feet on solid ground. "How long will ye be, then?"

"Let's see . . . It will take about half an hour to climb the steps," Colleen says. "More if the queue is long."

My mother looks aghast. "Half an hour of stair-climbing?"

"The Blarney Stone is part of the top tower," Colleen says, pointing at the turret looming behind the Woolen Mills.

My enthusiasm suddenly wanes. "Way up there?" I've never been a big fan of heights—or adventure, for that matter. Give me a comfy chair and a good book about someone else's adventures any day.

"Don't tell me you two are afraid of a little exercise," Colleen chides.

"Not at all," Annika says. "I have a personal trainer in L.A. It's the line I'm worried about. How can this pokey little town be so crowded?"

"Blarney Castle is one of Ireland's most popular attractions, missus," Lucky explains. "That's why people get here early."

The point is lost on Annika. For her, noon on Saturday is early. "Colleen, I hope you called ahead to say I was coming. I don't line up. Besides, this is my day off and I don't want to be pestered for autographs."

"You needn't worry about that, Missus," Lucky assures her. "None of the Irish film crew had even heard of you. Isn't that so, Colleen?"

Colleen quickly begins damage control. "Of course we knew of you, Annika, at least by reputation. But you're not yet a household name here as you are in America. Most of your shows air on the specialty networks that few people receive."

Annika is pouting. "You'd be surprised at how many people will recognize me when they see me. I believe that *Affair with a Werewolf* had quite a cult following all over Britain and Europe. At any rate, I am not climbing stairs in these sandals. We're taking the elevator and that's all there is to it."

Before Colleen can speak, Lucky jumps in. "It's the stairs or a magic broom, missus." My mother's eyebrows rise high above her sunglasses.

"What Lucky means," Colleen explains, "is that the castle hasn't been renovated since the fifteenth century."

Annika opens her bag and pulls out a scarf. "Off you go, then. I'll find a sunny bench and wait for you. Touch the rock for me."

"You don't touch it, Mother, you kiss it."

"Don't you dare kiss that thing, Vivien. It will be covered in disease. Touching it will more than suffice." She pulls a can of French mineral water out of her bag and mists it over her face. Then she produces a novel, her cigarettes, and a thermos before setting off across the landscaped grounds.

Something tells me Annika always intended to sit this one out.

★ ★ ★

"Are we there yet?" I ask Colleen, puffing.

"Stop your whingin' and climb. You're the one who wanted to come. I kissed the bloody thing ten years ago like any good Irish girl."

"Well, no one told me we'd have to climb Mount Freakin' Blarney."

"No one told you to wear a woolen school uniform in the middle of summer either."

"So far, summer in Ireland has been colder than winter back home. Who knew today would be decent? Besides, I'm trying to experience life as Sinead."

"You're going to experience life on the wrong side of Maude if you don't get that outfit back before she catches you."

Busted. But there's no reason to admit it, so I give her a nonchalant smile before peering over the outside wall of the castle to watch Annika on a bench far below us. She's smoking and talking on her cell phone. Even from here, I can tell by the tilt of her head that she's flirting. I suppose she's talking to Roger. Gross. If she marries him, I am not kissing him at the wedding. If I'm invited to the wedding, that is.

"Move along, girly," the man behind me says.

I pick up the pace, following Colleen higher and higher up the narrow, spiraling staircase. Eventually the stairs end and pick up again outside the tower walls. Here, they are slatted and I can see the long line of people below me. Good thing I'm wearing my cycling shorts. "Colleen, did I mention that I'm afraid of heights? I think I'll turn around and wait with Annika."

"Nice try, kid, but this route goes one way, and that's up. The way down is on the other side of the tower and you have to pass the Blarney Stone to get to it."

"Is nothing simple in this country?"

"Americans don't know simple when they see it."

Finally we emerge onto a platform that runs around the inside perimeter of the tower. Looking over the wall again, I see the tiny pink-and-blue speck that is Annika. She's still holding a phone to her ear and tossing her head around like a horse shaking off flies. I can almost hear the tittering from here.

"Nearly there," Colleen says, pushing me ahead of her.

"Great, where is it?" Now that the climbing is over, I'm able to feel excited again. I can't help hoping the stone glows, or at least gives off heat or something so that I'll know the magic is working.

"Right there." Colleen points to two young men lowering a very large woman to the floor of the tower. "They're holding on to her so that she can lean out and kiss the stone."

"What do you mean, 'lean out'?"

"The stone is outside the tower. Didn't you read the brochure I gave you?"

I am stunned into silence. A cheer rises as the men heave the woman back out of the hole and onto her feet. She passes us en route to the other staircase: there's no missing the monstrous cold sore on her upper lip. "Colleen, how many people a day kiss that stone?"

"Dunno, really. Maybe two hundred on a busy day?"

I shove her in front of me and tell the two guardians of the Blarney Stone: "I'm just here to support my friend."

One of them snickers. "Afraid of heights, are ye now?"

Colleen lowers herself quickly to the ground and sticks her head through the opening.

"I am not afraid," I tell the guys. "It's just that I have a cold and I'd hate to leave my germs on the stone to infect other people."

"Ye can't catch anything but a silver tongue from the Blarney Stone, it's enchanted. Right, Seamus?"

"Right, Malachy. We'd be dead by now if ye could. We kiss it every night before we leave."

"I don't believe you," I say. They're both very cute and if I weren't so terrified, I might even enjoy putting my life in their hands.

"It's true," Seamus says. "Helps us pull the birds."

"Colleen, you hold on to me, too," I say, when it's my turn. I sit down, careful to pull my jumper as low as I can before Malachy and Seamus guide me toward the hole. "These two might drop me."

"Never," says Malachy. "We only drop the ugly girls."

I'm still giggling as I lean backward over the edge of the castle. The stone juts out below me and I turn to lay a quick smack on the gray slab. There's no heat and no glow, but just the same, I feel a little different as the guys help me up. I sense my luck is about to change. But that could be the blood rushing to my head.

Turning at the top of the stairs, I wave good-bye to Seamus and Malachy. They throw kisses back. Colleen rolls her eyes and shoves me in front of her. "Move it, schoolgirl."

I don't care if it is a load of crap, I'm buying it, hook, line, and sinker.

★   ★   ★

Lucky hurries to the rescue when he sees Colleen and me staggering under the weight of my mother's purchases. For the past two hours, we've watched her try on dozens of outfits from Dublin's hottest designers at the Woolen Mills boutique. Now she is trailing behind us, empty-handed except for her purse.

"What a wonderful shop," Mom says, totally buzzed from her spree.

"You bought half their stock just because the sales clerk recognized you," I say, handing half a dozen bags to Lucky.

"Nonsense. You know how much I value my anonymity."

Yeah, about as much as she values a bad hair day. However, an afternoon of shopping and manicures puts Annika in such a good mood that she suggests dinner on the way back to Bray. Colleen recommends her local pub, Toner's, and though my mother hates pub food even more than regular food, she readily agrees. That is the power of a hand massage.

Lucky steps on the gas and we zoom back to Bray, arriving at Toner's Pub approximately five minutes before we left Blarney. The place is already bustling. Bartenders are shouting to each other over the loud Celtic music. In her heels, my mother has to stoop or risk scraping her big hair along the low ceiling. Stopping frequently to greet other regulars, Colleen leads us to a private booth in the corner called a snug.

The squealing begins before we've even picked up our menus. Several girls in the snug next to ours are standing to get a better look at someone.

"There, at the door: I think it's him," the first one says.

"Could be," another says. "I read in *The Tatler* that he's filming a movie near Bray."

"Yes, it's definitely Sean," the third says, firmly. "I'd know that brilliant butt anywhere." She's obviously the Voice of Authority.

In unison, the three scream: *"We love you, Sean!"*

Sean? Could it be *my* Sean? Nobody mentioned he has groupies. As I lean out of the snug to have a look, my head hits a denim-clad leg.

"If it isn't Sinead," the owner of the leg says, taking in my outfit. "Doing some character study on your day off, I see. I'm impressed!" I flush with pride. How great to connect with a fellow actor—especially this fellow actor. "D'ya think I could have my leg back, kid?" Yikes! I've been so enthralled that I didn't realize my head is still connecting with his thigh.

My embarrassment lasts only as long as it takes him to acknowledge the girls in the next snug and slide in beside my mother. I, Leigh Reid, am in a pub with Sean Finlay. Praise be to Blarney, my luck has finally turned. What are the chances that Sean would show up here of all places, just moments after we arrived?

"So you found the place all right?" my mother asks.

He nods. "My internal radar detects pubs with deadly accuracy. Hope you haven't been waiting long."

Haven't been waiting long? They must have set this up in advance, which is strange. Since when did they become such good pals? I suppose it's possible that she has clued into my love for Sean and invited him tonight to make me happy, but it's not like Annika to go out of her way for other people, especially me.

Offering to buy a round of drinks, Sean walks to the bar amid much squealing from the girls next door. Obvious, or what? Like Sean would ever fall for the desperate type. They're even louder as he returns carrying four pint glasses.

Sean slides one glass in front of me, which appears to contain beer. "Just to be sociable," he says.

Annika's alcohol detector goes off: "Sean, remember, she's fifteen." Like he could forget when people remind him every five minutes.

"Relax, Annie, it's a shandy—a little beer with a lot of ginger ale. I was practically raised on the stuff."

"And look at the good it did you," she says.

For once, Colleen agrees with Sean. "It's true, Annika, a lot of Irish teenagers drink shandies."

Finally, Mom gives a slight nod and I take a sip of the bittersweet brew. Then I rush to the bathroom and dig out my phone.

```
Abs,
I'm n a pub, drinkN
bER w Sean! wiL
fiL U n on Dtails
later.
Ireland roxs.
L
```

Colleen is at the bar talking to friends when I get back to the snug and Sean is leading my mother to the tiny dance floor. I'm surprised that Annika is following willingly, because she's never been much for dancing. She says it's undignified. The only time I saw her on a dance floor before, she stood in one place, immobile except for the occasional hair toss. Tonight, however, she is moving, because Sean is trying to teach her to step dance. As I watch from the sidelines, she stumbles off her heels, grabs Sean's shoulders, and giggles. Maybe the "undignified" line was a cover for the fact that she has two left feet. Sean doesn't appear to mind. In fact, he puts his hands on her waist to keep her from toppling and smiles as if he finds clumsiness charming. An alarm goes off in my mind. Annika is clearly flirting, but she flirts with everyone. Surely Sean would never fall for a fossil like her? She might be a beautiful fossil, but she's high maintenance. And if he thinks she hiked up all those stairs to lay a big one on the Blarney Stone today, he'll discover soon enough that she has no gift of the gab.

A voice behind me says, "You haven't got a chance, schoolgirl. Sean Finlay is too much man for a kiddie like you."

I look around to see the three girls from the next booth. We're all standing at the side of the dance floor doing the same thing: watching Sean. They're a scary bunch, with spiky dyed hair, supershort skirts, and belly-baring tops. Although they're not much older than I am, each has a pint of dark beer in her hand. I'm starting to regret the school uniform. How can I act tough while wearing mustard plaid? But then, *acting* is what this experiment is all about. So I look the ringleader right in the eye and say, "But you figure you're woman enough, I suppose?" It's a bold performance for a girl so outnumbered, but I figure if I can stand up to Roger, I can stand up to them.

"I am," the ringleader says, revealing a stud in her tongue. She's the one who commented on Sean's butt earlier, the Voice of Authority. "And I'm going to meet him, tonight, you can count on that."

"Big deal, I'm already dating him."

"Yeah and I'm married to Tom Cruise."

"Congratulations. I hope you're as close as we are. He just bought me a shandy."

Oops.

"A *shandy,* well, my mistake: you're all grown up and Sean knows it."

"Shut up." Obviously my gift of the gab has not yet arrived. No one mentioned a time lag.

"Count on a Yank for a clever comeback."

I try to get Sean's attention, but he is too intent on keeping my mother on her stilettos. The girls sneer and imitate me waving. I must look as desperate as they did earlier. This realization makes me turn and stalk back to our snug. The girls follow, continuing to taunt me.

"Excuse me, Lady Muck, but your boyfriend seems to fancy that aul' wan more than you," says the Voice of Authority.

"That old lady happens to be a movie star," I say, although defending my mother doesn't come easily to me. "And if you thought you stood a chance against her, you'd still be out there squealing at him."

"Shag off, gobshite," Authority says, making a move to grab my shandy.

I hold on to it for dear life. It may be years before I get another one. "Let go, you idiot. My father was obviously right about tongue piercings causing brain damage."

"Howya, girls?" We turn as one to see Sean, his white shirt and whiter smile dazzling in the dark pub. Behind him, my mother is watching from the edge of the dance floor, her arms crossed over her chest. Taking my hand, Sean pulls me over beside him. To Authority, he says, "You're not messing with my costar, are you?"

Authority's face crumples. "Your costar? That's a gas."

"I'm dead serious. She plays my sister in *Danny Boy,* my new film."

While Authority digests this, one of the other girls steps forward. "Would ye give us a dance, Sean?"

"Wish I could," he says, "but I'm spoken for tonight." Still holding my hand, he leads me to the dance floor, leaving the four girls with their mouths hanging open in disbelief. I give them a friendly wave, somehow resisting the urge to flip them the bird.

It's probably the happiest moment of my entire life—happier than when we brought Millie home and happier even than when Glen Myers asked me out. But the feeling only lasts a moment, because I soon notice my mother standing at the bar with a self-satisfied smile on her face. That's when it occurs to me that the rescue was probably her idea, not Sean's. Well, at least she had the sense not to come over herself and humiliate me even more. Either way, it was brilliant.

"Thanks, Sean," I say.

"It looked like you were holding your own against that bunch of wagons."

I don't know what a "wagon" is, but it sounds about right for Authority. "I guess, but it was three against one. Anyway, how did your dance lesson with Annika go?"

"Yer woman does try, but with those shoes, I practically had to prop her up."

I take this as a sign that he has not yet fallen for Annika's charms. I am so happy that I launch into the dance moves I learned during the hip-hop classes I took with Abby last year. Mom will deflate pretty fast when she sees that I have rhythm.

★　★　★

When the evil trio makes its next appearance, Colleen, Annika, and I are waiting at the door of the pub. Sean has gone to find Lucky.

Authority boldly demands, "I'd like your autograph."

My mother looks her up and down before saying, "I'm so sorry, but I don't sign when I'm off duty."

"I didn't mean you anyway," Authority says. "I meant *her*—Sean Finlay's costar." She waves a pen and a tattered coaster at me, and my mother's mouth falls open in shock.

"You want *my* autograph?" I can't help wondering if it's a trick.

"If it isn't any bother."

"Well, here's the thing. This lady, Annika Anderson, is the real headliner of *Danny Boy*. Not Sean, and not me. If she signs, I'll sign."

Authority turns back to Mom with her coaster. "Then how 'bout it, Mrs. Anderson? Please?"

"*Ms.* Anderson," my mother corrects her. But she takes the coaster and signs her name with a flourish.

When Authority hands it to me, I flip it over and write, *"Best Wishes—Yours Truly, Leigh Reid."* I'm about to hand the coaster back when I get an idea. After my last name, I add in brackets, *"Sean Finlay's Girlfriend."* Then I hand it back to Authority and quickly follow my mother out the door.

Once we're on the road, Mom says, "Put that Pink record on, will you, Lucky?"

I look at her in surprise. Not because she calls the CD a record—she always does that, no matter how many times I correct her—but because she only listens to classical music. Every time I ask if we can listen to one of my CDs, I get a lecture about the sensitive nerves of the artist.

Tonight, her nerves must be in good shape, because she is staring out the window with a slight smile on her face.

ten

I can hardly wait to get back to set on Monday morning. That's mostly because I'm excited about seeing Sean, but also because I'm looking forward to shooting new scenes. I've done my homework and I'm ready for anything. In fact, if Mom hadn't caught me studying the script by flashlight last night, I'd have memorized all the parts in *Danny Boy* by now. At 1 A.M., however, she woke up and confiscated my script, mumbling something about "insanity" and "beauty sleep."

Finian is in great spirits when we arrive in the makeup trailer. "It's the gorgeous Anderson girls," he says. "Walking, talking art."

In the interests of keeping our newfound peace, I don't bother to remind him that my last name is Reid.

My mother says, "Sounds like you've been kissing the Blarney Stone too, Fin."

"An annual pilgrimage is essential in my line of work," he says, rattling around in his drawers for the full brush complement. Mary and Maude step into action, wrapping plastic sheets around each of us. Finian winds a scarf around Mom's head to protect her hair before applying a thick, green paste to her face. "My special four-leaf clover healing mask," he tells me. "Very rare and very powerful. But don't get any ideas, Leigh, I never waste it on anyone under thirty."

"Hey," Mom mumbles through the stiffening goop.

"Right, I make an exception for your twenty-nine-year-old mother. Now, tell me all about your weekend."

As he works on Annika and Maud works on me, I tell about our trip. Mom occasionally chimes in, as her face mask permits, once laughing so hard that the green mask cracks like mudflats. Fin looks surprised that we're getting along so well.

"Has the legend kicked in yet?" he asks Mom, wiping the mask away with a wet cloth.

"If it has, she isn't wasting any blarney on me," Mom says.

"If I did, you'd never fall for it," I say.

The door hits the wall with a bang as Roger enters the trailer. Squealing, Mom hides her face in her hands.

"Roger," Fin says, indignantly, "you may be the director, but before you enter my kingdom, you must knock at the castle door."

"Er, right, Fin, sorry."

"Now, turn your back."

"I've seen Annika without her makeup before."

"Uh-uh . . . My kingdom, my laws."

Roger sighs. "It's lucky you're good, Fin. I wouldn't put up with this from—"

"I still see your lips moving, Roger . . . Turn, please."

He turns. "I'm really here to see the kid, anyway. May I look at *her?*"

"She can hear you just fine with your face to the wall, can't you, Leigh?"

"Yes," I chortle, delighted to see someone put Roger in his place.

"Don't laugh too hard, Vera," Roger says, "because you'll be back on my turf in ten minutes."

"Call time isn't for over an hour."

"We're reshooting the pub scene this morning, but before we head off on location, I want you to see the rushes."

"Rushes?"

"The film we shot Friday. It's a good learning opportunity for you."

My mother says, "I expect you'll want me there, too, Roger?"

"No need, darling. Besides, it looks like you could be a while."

Fin is outraged. "How dare you! Annika Anderson is one of the most beautiful women on screen today and you insult her? Out of my trailer! Out!"

"I'm done, anyway," Roger says. "Colleen will be back for you in eight minutes," he tells me. "Be ready."

The clover mask seems to have sapped the color from my mother's face and the freckles are standing out on her nose. She stares straight ahead at the mirror until Colleen collects me.

★ ★ ★

A dozen people have gathered in the small, darkened screening room, mainly the camera crew and some of the producers. I scan the room, disappointed when I see that Sean isn't here to share this big moment.

Wasting no time, Roger signals the technician to roll the film from Friday's pub scene. It's the first time I've seen myself on screen and I'm shocked. There's a bump on my nose that I never noticed before and my beauty mark looks like a beetle that might find its legs at any moment and take a stroll. There must be something wrong with the cameras, because my whole face is distorted. It can't be that long and narrow in real life. No amount of makeup is going to shrink *that* down to normal size. Maybe Fin can do something different with my hair to camouflage it.

I'm still riveted by the bump and the beetle when I notice that my lips are moving on screen. A shrill voice says, *"So you're Danny's birth mother. You've got some nerve to come back here after you abandoned him."*

Why didn't Roger tell me to lower my voice? I sound like a witch. No wonder "Fiona" is pushing her stool back from the table: there's a snarl on my face and it looks like I'm about to lunge at her. A bit of spittle flies out of my mouth and arcs across the table. I'm completely gross!

When it's over, Roger says, "Let's play that again."

"No!" I say. "I've seen enough."

Ignoring me, he signals to replay the scene. Again, I watch in horror as "Sinead" chews up the scenery, howling in rage.

"What do you see?" Roger asks me as it ends.

"I'm *awful*. My face is red and scrunched. It looks like I'm having some kind of attack, like I might—"

"Yes?"

"Like I might *bite* somebody."

Thank god Sean wasn't here. It's bad enough that he had to witness it firsthand. I hope I didn't spit on him.

"It's not *that* bad," Roger says. "But I wanted you to see how the camera captures your emotions before we shoot today's scenes. *Less is more*, kid, remember that."

Sinead needs anger management classes.

★ ★ ★

The scene we are shooting this afternoon takes place in the Wicklow Mountains, not far from Bray. It was scheduled for next week, but Roger seized the chance to move it up when the sun came out and the thermometer hit twenty-seven degrees. There was a sudden flurry on set as production staff organized a convoy of trucks, cast, and crew to pack up and move to our new location. My mother and I climb into Lucky's rocket and within seconds, the entire unit is little more than a speck behind us as we race toward a town called Glendalough. Since my mother is not in this afternoon's scene, I assume she is coming along to supervise. Or criticize.

In the scene, Sinead and Sean take a walk, just days before he is to leave for New York. He confesses to Sinead, as he can't to his parents, how he feels about everything that's happened since Fiona arrived. It's mainly a monologue on Sean's part, with Sinead looking sympathetic and nodding occasionally. My only line is: **"Don't worry, it will all work out."**

Surely I can handle that without turning into Cruella De Vil. The pub scene went all right this morning and my confidence is a bit higher. Just in case, I quietly repeat the words *less is more* as we drive along the winding coastal road. I have to rein in my emotion this afternoon. Otherwise, I might end up sobbing uncontrollably on the hillside as Danny discusses his sorrow at leaving his family. I've seen enough of these movies: he'll never come back. He'll forget all about his family when he gets to New York. Twenty years down the road, he'll show up expecting a big family reunion and they'll have practically forgotten him. He should just stay in Dublin where he belongs and save everyone a lot of trouble.

"What's that, darling?" Mom asks. "You're muttering."

"*Less is more*. That's what Roger told me this morning."

"It's true. Things always look bigger on screen, even the smallest gestures."

It's the closest she's come to acknowledging that, for this month at least, we are fellow actors. I could prolong the moment by asking her advice, but instead I say,

"Are you seeing Roger?"

"Uh, no, of course not," she says, clicking open her purse and rifling through it so that she doesn't have to look at me. "Why do you ask?"

"It seems like there's something going on between you, that's all. It wouldn't be a crime, you are single."

"Well, he's my director and that's never a wise move. Besides, *he* isn't single."

Surprised, I say, "He sure acts single."

"He's on his third marriage, actually. But, like many men—in this business anyway—he does enjoy the company of women."

"You mean he's a slime ball."

"It's not as simple as that. In real life, nothing is ever black and white. Like most people, Roger falls into the gray area. He's a very good director and he's an average man."

"Well, you don't need to settle for average," I tell her. My father isn't average.

She pulls a tube of Glazed Poppy lipstick from her purse and reapplies it. Something tells me this conversation is over.

⋆   ⋆   ⋆

Gravel pelts the bottom of the Audi as Lucky careens into the deserted church parking lot in Glendalough. Soon, this peaceful place will be transformed into the *Danny Boy* base camp. Vehicles of every kind will crowd the tiny lot and dozens of power cables will snake between the equipment trucks and trailers, like thick black licorice. Equipment will be unloaded and pushed by the cartload into the green hills beyond the church. Cast and crew will rush between set and the trailers, their hands full of scripts or tools or tea.

Lucky drops me in the churchyard and speeds off to take my mother on a cappuccino run to a nearby café. I find a picnic table and sit down to get in touch with my inner Sinead. Pulling my Discman from my knapsack, I select one of the CDs of Irish music that I bought at a gift shop in Bray yesterday and lie back on the warm wooden bench. Mentally, I'm already in an enormous farmhouse kitchen, where Sinead's grandfather and his friends are playing their instruments.

> *The entire O'Leary clan has gathered for a party. Sinead gets up to dance and soon Danny joins her. The rest of the family claps to the music as Sinead and her brother kick up their heels, rivaling Michael Flatley and his Riverdance troop. The music gets faster and faster. Danny spins Sinead around and around until she collapses in his strong arms and . . .*

I open my eyes and punch the stop button. Sinead O'Leary would never fantasize about her brother like that. Replacing the CD with the Corrs' latest, I close my eyes again and imagine myself at Sinead's school.

Sinead and her girlfriends have gathered in the gym locker room to help each other hitch up their skirts with their belts. The trick is to make the boring jumper more fashionable, while avoiding the wrath of the nuns who run the school. As the bravest of the group, Sinead hitches her skirt the highest. After all, she has a soccer-mad boyfriend named Aiden to impress. Recently, Sinead became the lead singer in a Corrs tribute band and it's about to play during half-time at the soccer team's semifinal match. Sinead is nervous, but once she's on the makeshift stage, she's feels right at home—like she was born to per- form. Aiden is watching from the front row in his soccer uniform. His thick, black hair stands on end over clear blue eyes and a warm, familiar smile. In fact, he looks very much like—

"Hey. You're thinking about that gack back home again, aren't you? I can tell by the smile."

I open my eyes to find Sean hovering over me, grinning. "I am thinking about Sinead's back story. Just like you told me."

Sean picks up a CD and asks, "Who the hell are the Paddy O'Neills?"

"The saleswoman said they're a popular Irish band." I snatch the CD out of his hand before he can see the photo on the back of gray-haired men and their fiddles.

"Not in Ireland they're not."

I wave another CD under his nose. "Well, the Corrs are popular."

"If you like that sort of thing."

"What about Westlife?"

"The boyband?" he snorts, unimpressed. "Danny O'Leary's sister listens to cooler music, write that into your back story. I'll bring some of my CDs and you can have a squizz."

"Really?" Nothing would make me happier than squizzing Sean's CD collection.

Colleen hollers from across the parking lot: "I've been looking everywhere for you two. You're overdue in hair and makeup. Move it, already."

Just when things heat up with Sean, Colleen always seems to ruin my fun. Grandma Reid has a word for her type: "killjoy."

★ ★ ★

If this is acting, bring it on. Sean and I have spent the afternoon on the sunny hillside, feeling the warm breeze in our faces and watching the sheep in the distance. The air is clear and fresh and wildflowers stud the grassy slope with splashes of indigo, white, and yellow. No wonder people rave about Ireland's beautiful scenery.

Each time Roger gives the signal, we stand and walk slowly toward the camera as Sean begins his monologue. It's nearly two pages of script and he keeps stumbling around the halfway point, causing Roger to start over. In two hours, we haven't even reached my line. It's getting harder and harder to focus on what Sean is saying. Instead, I find myself noticing how musical his voice sounds. When I glance up at him, I admire the sun gleaming on his glossy black hair.

"Cut!" Roger yells over the bullhorn as he wades through the brush toward us. "Kid!"

"What? I haven't even said anything yet."

"You *do* know Sinead is Sean's sister, don't you?"

"Yes." [sullenly] Of course I know that. I've read the script a hundred times.

"Well, quit fawning on him. It's pathetic."

"I am not fawning," I yell, stamping my foot silently on the grass. Was I?

Sean laughs and pats me on the back. "Roger, I should be so lucky. There's a Devin Bainbridge at home. A bit of a molly, though, from what I hear." He winks at me.

Roger ignores Sean. "Let's try it again without the fawning."

This exchange seems to have focused Sean, who nails the full monologue in the next take—only to have me stumble over my single line at the end. I'm so self-conscious now that I blow the next take as well. No matter how hard I try to feel like Sinead O'Leary, I can't stop feeling like humiliated Leigh Reid. Amazingly, Sean does not complain or tease me.

Before we can try again, Finian swoops up the hill, his caftan flapping in the wind.

"A moment, please, Roger," he calls.

"Make it fast," Roger says, "the light is fading."

"Scoot," Fin says to Sean, waving him away. "Leigh, let me powder your face. You're flushed. It looks like sunburn."

"Roger just embarrassed me."

"I know, Baby Doll, I was watching. He does that on purpose to help you stay in the moment."

"Well, he's made me so nervous I can't even say the line."

"Take a few deep breaths. That's the way. While Sean is speaking, you just focus on your breathing."

"Fin, can you cover my mole? It looks like a beetle."

"It does not look like a beetle. And no, Sinead can't suddenly lose her beauty mark midshoot. Roger isn't likely to write that into the script."

"What about my nose? A little contouring might help with the bump."

He takes a step backward and puts his hands on hips. "I absolutely forbid you to watch the rushes again if this is how you're going to carry on. You actresses are such a fragile lot." Slapping me on the backside, he glides over to the camera and stands behind it. *Breathe,* he mouths silently.

The next take, I focus on my breathing, careful to listen to Sean at the same time. Finally, just as I open my mouth to say my line, I plunge into a hole, lose my balance, and stagger against Sean. He throws an arm around my shoulders to steady me.

> DANNY
>
> Careful, sis. Almost went arse over tea-
> kettle there.

> SINEAD
>
> Who's going to catch me when you're gone?

> DANNY
>
> Don't worry, it's going to be fine.

"Cut!" Roger yells. "That's a wrap." He turns and walks down the hill.

I turn to Sean, confused. "We got the lines wrong," I whisper. "Did he miss it?"

Putting his arm around me again, Sean says, "Roger doesn't miss anything. He liked it."

Colleen and Finian crowd around us, giving me high-fives. I am so happy I almost float down the hill.

Mom and Roger are standing by the car when I get there. "Not bad, Velma," he says. Noticing my mother's disapproving expression, he adds, "A good save by Sean."

It *was* a good save by Sean. That's what comes of chemistry.

```
Abs,
Sean cn barely kEp
Hs h&z off me 18ly.
he's realizing dat
I'm perfect 4 him.
I c%d stNd living n Ireland.
It's d most BUTful country I've eva seen.
(bt I've onlE seen three).
L
```

eleven

The real action on a movie set happens during the downtime, when equipment is being moved and new scenes are being set up. That's when people talk, flirt, fall in love, start affairs, break up, and make up again. At least, so Colleen and Finian tell me. I miss it all, because my mother prefers to retreat to her trailer, accompanied, of course, by her personal assistant. While she rests or reads over her scenes, I organize her paperwork or perform any number of mundane tasks. Fin has taken to calling me Cinderella, but I figure it's worth it. Keeping Mom happy means she complains less about my involvement in *Danny Boy*. Besides, even Cinderella caught a break. One day, Sean may show up at the trailer door with a glass slipper in size ten.

Lately, I've learned more about Mom's life by setting up appointments in L.A. for her return. For example, I had no idea she had a shrink until I had to schedule her next round of visits. Nor did I know about her close relationship with Madame Hurrari, her psychic. In fact, Mom's typical day in L.A. consists of back-to-back bookings—yoga, personal training sessions, beauty treatments, lunches with her agent or directors, acting classes, and so on.

"Don't you ever just sit home and chill?" I ask.

"Being an actress is a full-time job, even when you're not working," she says. "An actress who 'chills' soon finds her career on ice."

"If it's such hard work, why bother? There are other things you could do."

I expect her to dismiss my question with an impatient wave, but she puts her script down and gives me her full attention. "Acting is all I've ever wanted to do," she says, "I made sure I didn't get any other skills so that there was nothing I could fall back on."

"Then why did you marry Dad if your acting career was so important?"

She sits up, as if I've just given her an opportunity she's been waiting for. "I was very young when I met your father in New York," she says. "He convinced me to join him in Seattle. He can be very persuasive when he wants to be, you know."

Uh-oh. This definitely has the sound of a prepared speech. Looks like I'm not the only one in the family who creates scripts in her head.

"I thought I could find work in Seattle," she continues, "but it just isn't a big enough film center. I could barely get a commercial. And when my acting coach said my career was as good as finished if I stayed, I believed him. I became very unhappy—and I made your father unhappy, too. I think he was glad to see me go."

If Dad were so thrilled to be rid of Mom, I expect he'd have replaced her with a human being as opposed to a cocker spaniel. Instead, he's had a series of casual girlfriends he's never brought home. Even I can see he isn't over her, although it sure beats me what's so unforgettable about Annika Anderson.

Not that I'm about to tell her that he's been pining for her for twelve years. No way.

"Well," I say, "I don't know if he was glad, but he didn't waste any time in getting a dog. Dee-Dee was great company."

She frowns at me. In her mental script, "Vivien" probably says something sweet and sympathetic.

"I wanted your father to come with me, you know."

Interesting. He never mentioned that.

"Oh yes," she says, as if I had delivered my line on cue. "He re-fused. He couldn't imagine giving up his stable job. Always so worried about money, your father—just like an accountant! As it happened, I got work right away—some trashy movie of the week, but I was happy to get it."

She pauses, clearly hoping I'll join this moving performance of *Annika's Story*, but naturally, I remain silent. After all, she's always blowing *my* mental scripts.

"The damage between us was already done," she says. "I did hope he'd change his mind and join me." There's another pause for dramatic effect, and then: "Maybe he hoped the same thing."

I get up and walk to the refrigerator trying to look bored be-yond belief. She needn't think I have the slightest interest in her feeble excuses. Getting the point, she concludes in a huffy tone, "That's the end of the story."

It might be the end of the story, but I notice the middle part is missing. The part I'm interested in. The part that included me. Af-ter all, Dad was probably worried about their income because there was a kid in the picture.

I could remind her of that fact, but why give her a chance to deliver more lines she's had a month, if not years, to write, revise, and rehearse? Better to ambush her later, when she's forgotten them. Judging by her acting, it will happen soon enough.

When I finally turn around, she's still watching me.

"Hey," I offer casually. "Did you know that Dad named Dee-Dee after your mother?"

She flings herself back on the couch and closes her eyes. "You're impossible."

I congratulate myself that I am. Then I pick up the phone and book an extra hour with her therapist for her first week back.

When I'm done, she's pretending to read. At least, I assume she's pretending, unless she finds hidden messages in *Persuasion* by reading it upside down and back to front.

★ ★ ★

Occasionally, I escape Mom's clutches between scenes and hunt Sean down. He's been quite nice to me lately and I'm finding it easier to speak to him in full sentences. If this keeps up, we may eventually have a real conversation.

Today I find him in his director's chair, reading *Persuasion*. It seems like an odd choice for a guy like Sean. The story is about a young heroine who gives up her true love on the advice of her mentor and soon regrets it. Ten years later, when she's almost over the hill, he comes back and gives her a second chance. This time, she makes her own decisions, marries him, and lives happily ever after.

"I can't believe you're reading Jane Austen," I say.

"What, you think I'm too much of a dunce to read Jane Austen?"

"No, it's just that my father says most men would rather run head-on into a wall of spikes than read her books."

"Well, he's never known a man of my civilized tastes."

"Then what do you think of *Persuasion*?"

Sean shrugs. "It's not half-bad. It's all about recovering from early mistakes and I like that—made enough of them myself. But I still prefer *Pride and Prejudice*."

"Me too!" I can't believe how much we have in common. "But Annika's obsessed with *Persuasion*. She's always trying to convince me it's the best. Like I'll ever change my mind about that."

"You'd be surprised what you can change your mind about. Did you come to Ireland wanting to act?"

"Definitely not."

"And yet, you may leave wanting to do just that."

I'm embarrassed. "I'd have to get a lot better before *that* happens."

"That's the problem with brainiacs," he says, reaching into his pocket to pull out matches and a long silver tube. "Never happy unless you're the best at something. The real fun is in the learning. Now, care to learn how to smoke a cigar?"

"Sure." I know he's kidding, but I call his bluff—mostly to see his eyebrows rise in surprise, but also because I've decided to take more chances in life. An actress needs to experience a lot of things so that she can draw on them when she's performing.

Not that I expect to land a lot of roles where cigar-smoking is required, but you never know.

★ ★ ★

When the coughing subsides and I no longer feel like throwing up, I hand the cigar back to Sean and turn my attention to the CDs he brought me. "The Pogues? Aren't they, like, *old?*"

Sean sends a puff of thick, blue cigar smoke my way. "Just because something is old, it isn't automatically lame. Keep an open mind and you might actually like it." He offers the burning stick to me again and I shake my head so hard that he laughs.

If Sean likes this music, I'll definitely give it a listen. It will give us something to talk about, now that we're becoming pals. I hold up the other CD, which has a picture of a young guy in a cowboy hat. "What's this one?"

"Something more recent. Yer man's a rising star here in Ireland. The girls all say he's juicy."

"Cool." You've got to like a guy who's confident enough to let you appreciate another guy's good looks.

Butting out the cigar and sliding it back into its tube, Sean says, "I'm impressed with the work you're doing to develop your character. If you like, I could bring in some books on acting."

"Sure, thanks." I try to sound blasé, but my heart is leaping around crazily, like Millie after a snowfall. First Sean brings me CDs and now he's offering books. I'm no expert on guys, but I know they don't go out of their way for anyone they don't like.

I'll read those books and do everything I can to improve as

an actress. With Sean's help, maybe I'll even win an award someday.

Scene 38: Leigh's Work Is Honored by the Academy

Leigh is sitting in the audience beside Sean, who looks absolutely amazing in his tuxedo. He gives her hand a squeeze and whispers, "Good luck, baby." A blond woman in a scarlet dress strides to center stage to present the award for best supporting actress. The presenter, Annika Anderson, reads the introduction, tripping over a couple of words on the prompter and giggling. One by one, each nominee flashes onto the big screen. A clip from Danny Boy *shows Leigh walking through the green hills of Ireland beside Sean. Below that, a real-time shot shows Leigh and Sean cuddling in the audience.*

ANNIKA
[opening the envelope]
And the winner for best supporting actress
in a drama is Leigh Reid—*my daughter!*

The crowd is cheering and Sean leans over to kiss Leigh on the mouth. The camera zooms in for a close-up.

SEAN
Way to go, beautiful! Knock 'em dead up
there.

LEIGH
I hope *you* win for best actor. Then the
night will be perfect!

*Leigh walks to the stage, climbing the stairs grace-
fully in her white, designer halter dress. She takes
the statuette from her mother's hand.*

ANNIKA

Darling, I am so proud of you. I cannot believe how good an actress you are. You absolutely deserve this!

LEIGH
[turning to the microphone]
I'd like to begin by thanking the Academy
for this award. Beyond that, my greatest
thanks go to my father, who raised me on
his own. I appreciate the endless support
of my wonderful fiancé, Sean Finlay, and
the best friend any girl could have, Abby
MacKenzie. Special thanks to my Irish support network, Finian Doyle and Colleen
Casey, and of course, to the director who
gave me my break, Roger Knelman. Thank
you, everyone.

*Leigh turns to leave the stage and Annika whispers
something in her ear.*

LEIGH
[stepping back to the mike]
I'm sorry, I'm so excited I forgot to thank
Annika Anderson, without whom I would
never have been on the *Danny Boy* set. Good
night!

It's lucky that Roger is in good spirits today, because nothing is coming together in this scene. Danny is supposed to yell at his adoptive mother, Kathleen, and storm out of the O'Leary kitchen while Sinead looks on, distressed. Kathleen then has a brief exchange with Sinead.

It takes hours to get the scene right, partly because of technical problems that range from the kitchen door's falling off to an electrical short that plunges the set into darkness. Amazingly, Roger just shakes his head and smiles. Someone must have shot him with a tranquilizer dart. I've taken advantage of the downtime to track down the dialogue coach. We don't just work on my lines, we chat about lots of things so that I can become more comfortable with the Irish accent. I think it's working, because I'm starting to feel less self-conscious about it.

Finally, Sean slams the repaired door successfully and Kathleen sits down across from Sinead at the kitchen table.

                    SINEAD
        You could stop him from going, Ma. All
        you'd have to do is ask him.

                    KATHLEEN
        It wouldn't work, luv. A boy his age always
        knows better than his mam. Besides, going
        to New York is the great adventure every
        young man would want. All you can do is
        let them go.

                    SINEAD
        I don't know how you stand it. Your heart
        must be breaking.

> KATHLEEN
> Children always break your heart. You'll
> find that out for yourself one day.

We do the scene many times and Roger remains calm, even when my accent temporarily returns to Liverpool. The fact that I recognize this myself and apologize seems to head him off at the pass. After that, I deliver my lines perfectly, but he seems to be looking for something that isn't there; I don't have a clue what it is.

We're so caught up that none of us sees the storm brewing on the sidelines until the winds reach gale force. Rising from her seat, my mother dramatically tosses her blue cashmere wrap around her thin shoulders and sails across the floor to Roger. His smile fades as he watches her approach.

"What is it Annika?" he asks. "You look annoyed."

"Of course I'm annoyed. Just how long are you planning on keeping me waiting for my scene?" she demands.

"A few more minutes, darling," Roger says, absently pushing her back toward her director's chair. "Go read a book. Or knit something."

This dismissal inflames my mother. "Knit something! Roger, I am the headliner in this movie, not some extra on a cattle call."

Roger's lips are moving silently as if he is counting to ten. "Sit down, Annika," he finally says. "Relax."

"Relax! Don't you tell me to relax! I have been sitting here in full makeup for five hours. Five! I have never been so insulted in my life."

Roger's patience has evaporated. "Darling," he says, "surely I've insulted you much worse. In fact, I *know* I have."

"Don't try to be funny, Roger. I was on time, like the professional I am, and you've kept me waiting endlessly while you repeat this trivial scene over and over."

"Trivial? On the contrary, Danny's relationship with these characters is critical. Caring about the nuances is what sets my films apart."

Four weeks into this film, I've heard Roger's eerily calm tone often enough to know that there's danger ahead. Sean knows it too, because he steps back onto set and glances warningly at my mother.

Staging a rescue attempt, I say, "Listen, Annika, how about—"

Shushing me with an impatient gesture, she continues, "Spending time on brief scenes with minor characters is what pushes you over budget."

"So you're an expert on direction, now, are you?" he asks.

"I know inefficiency when I see it."

"How about keeping your eyes on the mirror, where they usually are?"

"Well, at least I'm not leering at anyone."

Roger's eyebrows gather in a frown, making me want to run for cover. "Who'd notice if you did, darling? You're just another aging diva."

Mom turns a mottled shade of eggplant. "How dare you!"

"Let's face it, Ann, you were nearly washed up when I cast you in *Danny Boy* and if this isn't a hit, it could be the last film you ever do."

"I have my best years ahead of me, you bastard, but I won't waste them on you. You'll still be finishing this film anyway."

"Look, we both know what this is about. It's about Viola."

"Well, since you brought it up, I think it's pathetic that you're spending so much time doting on someone young enough to be your granddaughter. You can't even get her name right."

"What's pathetic, darling, is that you are so jealous of your own daughter that you'd try to sabotage her opportunity."

My mother is silent, her chest heaving in rage. Clearly she thought she had Roger fooled about the sister act.

"Yes, I know she's your daughter," Roger continues, "and I know you're terrified that she might have more talent than you have."

"I am not!"

"You are. And she might. Why don't you go back to your chair and let me find out?"

He flicks his fingers at Mom as if she's an annoying gnat. Something in her seems to snap. Taking a step toward Roger, she hurls her script. It hits him in the chest and falls to the floor with a thud.

Colleen lunges forward and grabs Mom's arm, but she shrugs her off and storms to the edge of the soundstage. There, she turns, perhaps expecting to see Roger coming after her. When she sees he's still standing beside me, she seems to deflate. In fact, at this distance, she looks like a little girl.

"Focus, everyone," Roger says, casually kicking the script aside. "Let's try this again."

When I look again, Mom has disappeared.

It doesn't take long after this to nail the scene. Roger must be distracted, however, because he doesn't seem to notice that my eyes are watering a bit as I say my last line.

★ ★ ★

Colleen swoops down on me at wrap. "Good work today, kiddo. I'm heading over to Toner's Pub. Are you on for a bite?"

The offer is tempting, but I say, "I think there's a quiet night in Bray on my schedule."

"I've already told your mother that you're coming with me; she didn't say no."

"Did she say *anything*? Or is she rocking quietly in a corner of the trailer?"

"Since when did a teenager care about details? Anyway, the poor woman could use some time alone."

We climb into Colleen's vintage Mini Cooper and careen at high speed to Toner's. Although there's a group from the *Danny Boy* crew at the bar, Colleen steers me to a table. She says it's so we can see the stage, but I know it's really because the hot topic of the night will be my mother's fight with Roger. She fetches our drinks from the bar and lets me try her Guinness. I may be mature beyond my years, but I am not mature enough to like that vile, black brew.

Eventually, a pale blonde steps onto the stage and the crowd falls silent. She sings a very long, very sad song about lost love and her beloved country. Although she has a nice voice, for some reason I find myself wanting to laugh. Maybe it's hysteria building after a tough day.

"Don't laugh," Colleen whispers, her own mouth twitching.

"But everyone's taking it so seriously."

"Of course they are. This is a time-honored Irish tradition."

"If she mentions the potato famine, I'll lose it, I swear."

When the song finally ends, I turn to Colleen and say, "It was awful."

She knows I mean the fight, rather than the song. "Your mother and Roger are always milling," she says, soothingly.

"It was so humiliating." I mean for my mother, not me, and Colleen knows that, too.

"Actresses and directors are combustible. It's part of the package."

"He didn't have to be so mean."

"No, he didn't. There's probably more to it than we're seeing."

Sounds like she also suspects Annika and Roger have had a relationship. It's too disgusting to think about right now, so I change the subject. "Do you think Roger is right about Annika being jealous of me?"

"Probably, but who could blame her? There she is, career peaking and you start out by walking right into a part."

"I want to be a vet anyway."

"If you succeed without trying, it's even worse."

"I am trying," I say. We sip our drinks in silence for a moment before I get the nerve to ask, "Colleen, do you think I have any . . . uh, potential?"

"I'm no expert, but I think so. You'd have to commit to it, though. It's not something you can mess about with on summers off from your veterinary practice."

"I don't think acting is really for me. I'm just curious."

"Well, play it cool while you think about it. Your ma will come around. She's not a bad woman."

Before I can share *my* views on that subject, Sean walks through the door of the pub. He waves to us and weaves his way through the crowd toward the bar. I lean back on my stool at a perilous angle to check out his butt.

"Give it up, girl," Colleen says.

"What do you mean?"

"You know what I mean. Sean is not the man for you."

"I think he is," I say, defiantly.

"He's six years older than you are and it might as well be a hundred."

"You don't know how much we have in common. He can see past my age."

"Some men might see past your age, but Sean is not creepy enough for that, thank god."

"I can take care of myself, Colleen."

"Fortunately, you don't have to. I just don't want you to be hurt when you realize . . ."

"Realize what?" Sean interrupts, sitting down beside Colleen.

"What a big wanker you are," she tells him.

"Oh, she knows already, Colleen. Told her myself to avoid surprises."

Colleen and I both laugh, but Sean seems distracted. He keeps scanning the pub, as if expecting someone. Meanwhile, he lifts his pint and drains it with a few effortless swallows.

"Unbelievable," Colleen says.

Sean burps and wipes his mouth on his sleeve. "A man of many talents," he tells her. To me, he says, "So, Annie's your ma, then."

"You didn't know?"

He shakes his head. Surely he was the only one on set who hadn't figured it out. "Where is she?" he asks.

Colleen says, "Sent her home early for a good night's sleep."

"Could use one myself," he says, "but I'll join the lads awhile first."

He slaps me on the shoulder and heads over to the bar, leaving me to gaze after him, discouraged. Colleen gives me a "what did I tell you" look. The only reason she's not saying it out loud is because she thinks I've suffered enough for one day.

★   ★   ★

I expect Mom to be hiding under the covers when Colleen drops me off at the cottage, but I find her sitting in the kitchen with Mrs. O'Reilly. The whiskey bottle on the table between them is empty; the ashtray, on the other hand, is full.

"Mrs. O'Reilly," Mom slurs, "did you know that my daughter is going to be a fine actress one day?"

"Is she now?" Mrs. O'Reilly says, around the two cigarettes in her mouth.

"She is."

"Well, she has a fine example before her," Mrs. O'Reilly says. Maybe it's my work with the vocal coach, but I have no problem understanding Mrs. O anymore.

"You're too kind! Now, will you give us another song?"

Mrs. O'Reilly removes the cigarettes, places them carefully in the ashtray, and begins warbling "Danny Boy."

"Oh my, that won't do at all, will it, darling?" Mom says to me in a pig's whisper. To Mrs. O'Reilly she says, "I hate to interrupt when you're in such good voice, Mrs. O, but Vivien just asked to hear you play your fiddle."

Actually, I hadn't even noticed it on the chair beside her. But Mrs. O'Reilly stops singing, replaces the cigarettes in her mouth, and tucks the fiddle under her chin. She strikes up a rollicking tune, eventually shaking a column of ash onto the instrument. Long before the song is done, my mother begins applauding loudly.

"Mom," I say, "maybe you should go to bed."

"Not yet. Mrs. O is helping me sort out the Roger issue."

"The curse of the crows on him," Mrs. O mutters.

"That's the spirit," Mom says, giggling. "She cannot believe how Roger abused me today. Another curse, Mrs. O."

"May the cat eat him and may the cat be eaten by the devil," Mrs. O says.

"Excellent! The devil is exactly what he deserves."

I walk around the table and take Mom's arm. "Come on, Annika, time for your beauty sleep."

"One more for good measure, Mrs. O. Give it your all."

"May he be afflicted with the itch and have no nails to scratch with," Mrs. O offers triumphantly and resumes playing.

"Perfect! A nasty, itching disease. See what you can arrange, will you, while I get some rest? Talk to those little friends of yours." As I lead Mom into the bedroom, she whispers, "Mrs. O has some pull with the leprechauns, you know."

I climb into my cot and lie awake for a long time, listening. Mrs. O'Reilly certainly has more talent with a fiddle than a fry pan.

twelve

Mom snores right through the alarm when it rings at 7 A.M. Realizing that she has a rude awakening ahead, I decide to bring her a cup of tea. Pretty thoughtful of me, considering the personal assistant is off duty. My love for Sean must be making me soft.

I walk into the kitchen to find Mrs. O'Reilly exactly where I left her last night, only now she's slumped over the table, sound asleep. Worn out from all that cursing, I suppose.

By the time I've knocked the kettle against the faucet a few times (entirely by accident), Mrs. O is stirring.

"Bloody hell," she says. "Feel like I've had a bad dose."

"Well, a *big* dose anyway—of whiskey."

Slipping her bare feet back into her boots, she heaves herself upright, smoothes her rumpled housedress, and shuffles over to the stove.

"Fry up?" she asks, briskly, as if it's breakfast as usual.

"Let's just have toast today," I suggest. "The smell of bacon might make Mom barf."

Ignoring me, Mrs. O turns on the heat under the cast iron frying pan and opens the refrigerator.

"That director of yours is a bad egg," she says, laying strips of fatty bacon in the pan with nicotine-stained fingers.

"He's tough, but Mom kind of asked for it yesterday. She threw a tantrum."

"Still, there's no call to talk the way he did." She turns to give me a baleful glance and adds, "You're not much better yourself."

"Me!"

"Always with the puss on you, always giving her cheek."

The nerve! My mother may look like a delicate flower, but she gives as good as she gets. Besides, I am the one who's been wronged for the past twelve years. I could tell her all about that, but I am above slagging off my family to near-strangers. I have class. In fact, the scenery along the high road is becoming very familiar.

"Mrs. O'Reilly," I say with dignity, "you do not know the whole story."

Shaking a greasy finger at me, she says, "This I know: you only get one ma, youngwan."

"Yeah, well I'm still waiting for the other half of mine to arrive. The Diva Depot is totally backed up."

Mrs. O studies me for a moment before replying. "That'd be the cheek I mentioned." She takes the teapot out of my hand and waves me away. "Go on with you. I'll wet the tea myself. You Americans don't know how to make a decent cuppa."

I take my dignity into the next room, where Mom is lying on her back pretending to be asleep. There are dark rings under her eyes and her curls are matted on the pillow.

"Time to get up," I tell her, my voice a little louder than necessary. No response. "Mom, I know you're awake. Call time is at nine, so you'll have to hurry."

I sit down on my cot and stare at her until she finally opens her eyes and croaks, "I'm not feeling well."

"You have to go to work: you're the headliner."

"Tell that to Roger," she says, rolling onto her side and curling into the fetal position.

"Come on, Mom. The show must go on."

"I am not leaving this cottage until five-dozen yellow gladiolas arrive." I laugh out loud. "I am not joking, Vivien," she says lifting her head to glare at me. "He knows they're my favorite. In fact, I'm not getting out of bed for less than six dozen and you can tell him that."

"I'm not telling him anything. This is between you two."

"He brought the whole cast and crew into it yesterday." She covers her eyes with her arm and groans dramatically.

I'm about to remind her that she was the one throwing things when it occurs to me that I might be able to use her weakened condition to get some straight answers out of her. "So," I say, trying to sound casual, "at the pub last night, people were saying you're having an affair with Roger."

Suddenly alert, she moves her arm to look at me. "Who said that?"

"Lots of people."

"He should be so lucky, that monster."

I notice her eyes have drifted to my left shoulder. "Well, is it true?"

"It most certainly is not true." She pulls the sheet over her head and mutters something that sounds like, "Not anymore."

"Mom, I heard that. When did it end?"

Avoiding the question, she mumbles, "He directed me in *The Lady of the Thistle* ten years ago, you know. It was the best role of my career, next to *Danny Boy*. I thought he was an absolute genius and . . . Well, you know how it is."

I have no idea how it is. Maybe she finds his supposed genius enough to make up for his other shortcomings. "I hope he was nicer to you then than he is now."

She throws back the sheet with a sigh. "Not much. We were on and off for years until he dumped me for the little tart he married. She's not much older than Colleen. I know that he doesn't love her; he just likes having a trophy wife." Mom closes her eyes and rubs her temples. "I think your father is the only decent man I ever loved."

Although she's feeling plenty sorry for herself today, the conversation doesn't sound scripted, so I can stand it a bit longer. "If Roger treats you that way, why did you take *Danny Boy*?"

"You have to ask? It's a feature film with a great script backed by a big studio. I thought playing Fiona would help me make the transition to more mature roles. I knew I was practically washed up. I didn't need Roger to tell me so—or to call me old and ugly."

"He never said ugly." Even pale and pouting, she's far from ugly. "Remember what Fin said—that you're one of the most beautiful women on screen today. And he's in a position to know."

She brightens slightly. "He is, isn't he?" Her face crumples again a second later. "What use is beauty? It's too late for me now," she whispers.

It's my turn to sigh. I haven't had much experience handling wounded divas, but if I want to get to set today, I'll have to try harder. I can't bear the thought of explaining to Roger and Sean that Annika has taken to her bed. "Mom, Roger wouldn't have cast you as the lead in *Danny Boy* if he didn't think you had talent. He obviously doesn't do anything just to be nice."

"He thought I had talent ten years ago. In fact, Roger might be the only one who ever really saw my gift. But it all came to nothing."

"You've had dozens of roles—and you've made lots of money. That's something."

"It's not about money. It's about feeling like you didn't deliver on your potential." She hoists herself onto one elbow to make sure I'm paying attention. "At your age, no one believes it will all end at forty, but that's how it is in Hollywood."

"Oh come on, lots of actors make it big after forty."

"Character actors, maybe. Not leading ladies."

"So you'll be the first. Maybe you'll do your best work playing mothers—or even grandmothers."

I'm trying to be encouraging, but her face grows even paler at the mention of grandmothers.

"Just kill me now and get it over with," she says, throwing herself back on the pillow.

It's tempting. With that pillow and my healthy BMI, I could finish the job in minutes. But that would be the end of my cinematic career—and a romance with Sean that's close to lift-off. Better to take one more whack at this pep-talk business. "Look, the other day you said that acting is all you've ever wanted to do. *Acting*—not playing the movie star, not being a celebrity. If that's true, you shouldn't be afraid of taking smaller, more interesting roles if they challenge you."

"You mean in independent films?" she asks, grimacing.

"Why not? If *Danny Boy* is a hit, there may be other offers from big studios, but in the meantime, why not take a risk? That's what Grandma always tells me."

"Indie films won't pay for veterinary school." She sits up, takes the hairbrush from the bedside table and starts working it through her tangled mop. I must be making some headway.

"Of course, your looks would be totally wasted in indies," I say. "Don't they use quirky-looking actors? Maybe you could lose a couple of teeth."

She glances over at me and smiles for the first time today. "Not to worry, you'd be amazed what harsh lighting can do."

In the kitchen, Mrs. O'Reilly is rattling cutlery to let us know that breakfast is ready and not a moment too soon because I'm already exhausted. "Okay, Mom, out of bed. Fin may need extra time with you today."

"What do you mean by that?" she asks, testily.

"Well, you need to look your best. You have to let that Roger know you don't give a damn what he thinks."

"Right. Of course." She sounds unconvinced. "I'll try."

"Don't just try, Mom, *do it*. Act if you have to. Think of it as an audition for your new indie career."

My hand is twitching to slap some sense into her. Mrs. O must pick up on the vibes, because she pushes open the door without knocking and plods into the bedroom. She takes my mother by the elbow and hoists her off the bed. Still in her designer pajamas, Mom meekly trails after Mrs. O into the kitchen.

★　★　★

Once we're on set, there's help to keep Mom afloat. Fin, having been warned in advance by Colleen, kicks the flattery into overdrive the moment he sees her. He does everything but compose a sad Irish song about Annika's beauty. The poor man will need a special trip to Blarney Castle this weekend to replenish his supply.

Despite Fin's efforts, Mom is a bundle of nerves, wobbling along beside me on her four-inch heels. Her hand shakes as she brings a teacup to her mouth and the slightest noise startles her. If this keeps up, I'll have to ask Colleen to hook us up with the local shrink. By the time we're on set, however, she seems calmer.

"Break a leg," I whisper as her scene is called.

When Roger beckons, she takes a deep breath, rises from her seat and strides toward him, looking confident. Acting opposite Danny's "parents," she delivers her lines perfectly. She turns to Roger with a serene smile.

"Right on the mark, Annika," he says, sounding surprised. "Your accent is flawless today."

"Thank you," she says, her voice icy. "I had a crash course with a local expert last night."

She's so pleased with herself that she practically skips back to her chair. "That'll show the wanker," she tells me.

"Mother, how vulgar!"

I give her a high five, which she misses, and we both giggle as Roger watches curiously.

★　★　★

Back in the trailer, the euphoria soon wears off. Mom still has a couple of tough scenes with Sean ahead of her and she's anxious. I offer to fetch a cappuccino.

"No, stay here," she says, clutching my arm. This needy routine is getting tired.

"If I go to craft services, I can find out what people are saying."

"I don't care what people are saying." There's a note of hysteria in her voice.

"You might not care, but if we knew, we could work on some good lines to feed them."

She ponders this argument just long enough for me to slip out the door.

I'm only a few yards from the trailer when Sean appears, carrying a long white box. "Howya, kid," he says. "How's your ma?"

"She's fine. What's in the box?"

He sets the box on the stairs and removes the lid: a dozen yellow gladiolas. "I thought they might cheer her up," he says.

My breakfast takes a slow, unpleasant turn in my stomach. This is totally unfair. How come Mom gets to throw a tantrum in public and then be coddled and flattered by everyone? Meanwhile, I mouth off to Dad once and get sent away for the summer. "You're five dozen short," I say. "She said this morning she wasn't coming back to set for less than six."

His face falls. "Well, she's here," he says, shrugging. "Roger will have to give her the other five."

"That's what she had in mind." My voice is sharp because I am furious that he has gone to so much trouble for her. Yellow gladiolas are practically nonexistent in Bray at this time of the year. I should know: I've had to track them down several times to brighten her trailer. How does he know what her favorite flower is? And why does he care? I would like to take that big white box and throw it. Not at Sean, but at the trailer, where Mom is probably listening behind the door.

"You're right narky this morning," he says.

"I just think it's stupid that people are tiptoeing around my mother as if she's a—"

"—a high-strung bit of talent?"

"Exactly. She gets away with murder."

"Beautiful women always do. It's a fact of life. Anyway, is she inside?"

"Check for yourself. I'm not *your* personal assistant."

"Oh, dry your arse, ya babby."

My mother opens the trailer door and leans weakly against the doorframe. "Stop it, you two. My nerves cannot take another harsh word."

This from the woman who was shrieking like a banshee yesterday.

"Sorry, Annie," Sean says, firing a thousand-watt smile in her direction. "Your daughter doesn't have your winning personality."

"Well, she's a lot like her father," Mom agrees.

So this is the thanks I get for bolstering her ego all morning. I've got to stop being so nice all the time.

Sean points to the flowers and says, "For you."

"How lovely, Sean!" Her gushing makes me want to gag. "You shouldn't have. Leigh, put these in a vase, will you?"

"What did your other slave die of?" I cross my arms across my chest in a show of defiance.

"Pardon me?"

"I said—"

"I heard what you said." She cuts me off with a threatening growl. "I am asking you as my *personal assistant*."

"Fine."

I flounce over to the stairs to pick up the box, but Sean picks it up first. He selects a single stem and, with a bow and a flourish, offers it to me.

"A peace offering," he says.

My mother is beaming, which only infuriates me more. I turn to sweep away haughtily—and find Colleen standing behind me, hands on her hips. I don't know how much she has witnessed, but her expression suggests I'm becoming more like my mother by the day. I feel myself shriveling like a balloon the day after a birthday party. Turning back, I reach out to take the flower from Sean's hand, forcing my lips into a smile. "Thank you," I say. "It's beautiful."

It's the best bit of acting I've done yet.

★ ★ ★

"Leigh? Is that you?"

I am trying Sinead's accent out on my father. "'Tis indeed."

"Something must be wrong with the phone line. Your voice sounds funny."

Dad really needs to leave his desk more and experience the world. Dropping the accent, I ask, "Do I sound better now?"

"I was teasing, Sprout. You've always been good with accents. But you didn't call to practice on me. What's wrong?"

Dad hasn't called me Sprout for years, but hearing it now is comforting. After acting like a parent to my mother all day, it's nice to be the kid again. Good thing I didn't fire him.

"Nothing's wrong. I just figured you'd be missing me, so I picked up the phone."

"Well, that's a first."

"I guess things have been kinda harsh around here lately, that's all." I'm about to launch into the story, when Mom comes out of the bedroom. "Hang on a sec, Dad." I put a hand over the receiver.

"I just wanted to say good night," she says. "I'm so exhausted that I'll probably be asleep by the time you're off the phone. Leigh, I know I was a bit difficult today." A bit difficult? That's like saying history class is a bit boring. "But I did appreciate your support, darling, and I promise I'll be my cheerful self by morning."

That might be a stretch, but since Dad can probably hear some of this, I say, "Okay, good night."

Still she won't go. Stepping toward me, she holds out a small gift bag. As I reach for it, she leans forward quickly to kiss my cheek. I make an effort not to flinch that isn't entirely successful.

"I don't bite, darling," she says, giggling. "Now, don't stay up too late. And say hi to your dad for me."

I watch her disappear into our bedroom and put the phone back to my ear. "Sorry about that, Dad."

"No problem. Now, what's bothering you, kiddo?"

I peek into the bag and find the latest issues of *Jane* and *Elle Girl*. That's weird, something I actually like. "Oh, nothing."

"But you said things have been harsh."

"It's just been raining a lot. And I miss you and Gran and Millie."

"We miss you too." He fills me in on the battle of the pets, which Percival is apparently winning. "Anyway," he concludes, "I'm glad you're okay, Sprout. I worry about you."

"Dad, we talked about the 'Sprout' thing. I'm not a kid anymore. And you don't have to worry about me."

A series of particularly loud snorts rattles the cottage. For a second, all is silent and then Annika's snoring resumes.

"Hey, I can hear the thunder," Dad says.

"I told you. The bloody sun never shines."

"Watch your language," he says, but I can tell he's smiling.

"Good night, Da. I really am fine."

thirteen

Mrs. O'Reilly has left to spend a few days in Cork with her sister, who is recovering from hip surgery. Right up until the last minute, she threatened to cancel the trip, because she was so worried that we couldn't cope on our own. Finally we managed to herd her out of the cottage and into the car, where I caught a glimpse of her good dressing gown beneath her raincoat as she settled into the driver's seat. Now Mom and I are left to fend for ourselves, which should be interesting, since neither of us cooks. Of course, only one of us eats and I can get some of my meals on set. It will be nice to have some variety. As much as I like her soda bread, Mrs. O is way too attached to her frying pan for my liking.

When we get to set, I join the line running alongside the catering truck. "What'r ye havin', then?" a voice bellows from the window.

I look up to see a bald man wearing a stained apron over a dingy tank top. "Uh, what are you serving?"

"Fried eggs, fried tomatoes, fried bread, fried mushrooms, sausages, black puddin', and chips."

"Uh, do you have anything that isn't fried?"

"Oatmeal. Help yerself." Flashing a hairy armpit, he points his spatula toward an enormous vat of porridge.

The steel ladle bends as I scoop porridge into a bowl. Holding out her hand for the ladle, Colleen says, "It's not bad, once you add a little salt."

"Salt? Gross!" Turning back to Hairy Pits, I ask, "Could I have some maple syrup, please?"

"Well, if it isn't the Queen of Sheeba," he says, for the benefit of the people in line. "She fancies *maple syrup* this morning, she does. Well, missy, this is a catering van, not the Ritz. The salt's beside the porridge."

"How about giving me a hand with the extras today?" Colleen asks, joining me at the coffee and tea table, where I am covering my oatmeal with milk and sugar. "It's going to be crazy."

Annika has ordered me to spend the day tracking down a rare collagen cream from Sweden, so I waste no time in saying, "Sure, why not?"

★ ★ ★

We're on location at the estate of Lord Tracy, whose family has been brewing Irish beer for centuries. The beautiful grounds have been transformed for the day into a small amusement park. As a reward for helping to send extras through the scene at carefully timed intervals, Colleen lets me ride the Ferris wheel when the sun pokes through the clouds. I still don't like heights, but the view of the surrounding countryside is worth it.

Finally it's time for my transformation into an Irish Catholic schoolgirl. I head over to Fin's trailer, where a pleasant surprise awaits: instead of my usual wool uniform, there's a gorgeous, pale blue sundress with spaghetti straps and glittering silver embroidery on the bodice. The skirt has layers of sheer material, each a little shorter than the one below.

"Isn't it grand?" asks Maude.

"Isn't it brilliant?" asks Mary.

"We found it at a vintage shop this morning."

"We had to go into town for yer ma. Yer woman didn't like her frock for today."

"We raced around the shops as soon as they opened to buy her a new one."

"And then we spotted this for you."

"It's perfect for today's scene."

"Do you like it?"

Mary and Maude volley their comments so quickly that it's almost like talking to one person. "I love it!" I say, pulling off my jeans and sweatshirt. "But isn't Sinead supposed to be coming straight from school to the park?"

"Not necessarily."

"There's a time cut."

"It's early evening in the scene—"

"—so she could be coming from anywhere."

"It's a grand fit!"

"You look spectacular!"

As they spin me in front of the three-way mirror, I can't help but agree with them. The dress shows off my small waist and strong arms and even shows a hint of cleavage. Most important, it makes me look older.

"Who's the model?" Finian asks, stepping into the trailer.

"Isn't this the most wicked dress ever?" I give a spin and plop into Fin's chair, holding out one foot with its matching blue platform shoe for his inspection.

"All you need is a glass slipper, Cinderella. Let's put your hair up."

Tunes blare, brushes wave, and glittery hairpins fly. Half an hour later I emerge feeling very much like a princess. Sean Finlay can't help but lose his heart to me today.

Danny Boy, Scene 14

The sun is setting over the amusement park and few people remain on the quiet grounds. Danny is sitting alone on the slowly spinning carousel. As Sinead approaches, he is so deep in thought that he doesn't notice her.

SINEAD
So this is still your secret hiding place.

DANNY
I guess it's not as secret as I thought.

SINEAD
[stepping carefully onto the moving platform]
It's secret enough: Da and Mam don't know
about it and I'll never tell.

Sean smiles at me and I can't help thinking Danny is admiring his little sister more than he usually does.

DANNY
I come here when I need to think.

Sinead watches Danny for a moment, studying his face for clues.

SINEAD
What's wrong, Danny? You haven't been
yourself lately.

DANNY
I know, I'm sorry. I've got a lot on my mind.

SINEAD

Who is she?

Danny is silent for a minute. He didn't realize that anyone knew about Fiona. He considers lying to Sinead, but somehow she always sees through him.

DANNY

She's my mother.

"Cut! Print!" Roger yells. "Well done, kids. And in one take, no less."

I look over at Roger and see my mother standing beside him. Her scene ended an hour ago and I thought she'd already be in Fin's trailer, scraping off the war paint. She hardly ever watches my scenes anymore. Maybe she's turning over a new leaf.

"Do *not* call me 'kid,'" Sean says, stamping his foot in a pouty imitation of me. "I am twenty-one and I am all grown up."

My mother and Roger both laugh and even I have to grin.

"You're still the second youngest person on set," Roger points out. "And it's our Sinead who looks twenty-one tonight. Darling, you look radiant! Absolutely delectable!"

Radiant is good. Delectable, not so good. My mother clearly doesn't think so either because she has stopped laughing to watch Roger with narrowed eyes.

"Be careful, Roger," Sean says, "or you'll give the kid an even bigger noggin than she already has. There's barely room for it in the trailers now."

"Well, when you look like her, vanity is allowed," Roger says. "That dress is worthy of an introduction of the Queen, but she'll have to settle for a lord tonight."

"What do you mean?" I ask.

"Lord Tracy invited us to the manor for cocktails after wrap."

Roger looks over his shoulder at my mother and adds, "You can come too if you like, Annika."

★   ★   ★

It took ten minutes of begging and a promise to do the cast's laundry for a week if I spill anything on it, but Mary and Maude finally agreed to let me wear the blue dress to the cocktail party. My mother slips into a red silk dress the precise shade of her Glazed Poppy lipstick and gets Finian to do her hair again. She looks more beautiful than ever, but she's in so foul a mood that even Fin can't lift it.

I, on the other hand, have been taken over by the spirit of Cinderella, thanks to everyone's reaction to the dress. I can't wait to get to the ball and meet his Lordship. "Where's my pumpkin coach?" I say, as we step down from the trailer. Fin, Mary, and Maude are laughing as they head off to collect the rest of the crew. Since Mom doesn't crack a smile, I make it my mission to cheer her up during our trek through the fields. This is a huge event in my life and I don't want her whining to leave the moment we get there. "Why aren't you more excited, Mom? Have you ever met a lord?"

"Not that I recall," she says, "but it's only a title, you know. I'd be more excited about meeting Katharine Hepburn."

"No kidding. That's because she's already dead."

"You get my point. Lord Tracy didn't have to accomplish anything to become a lord,"

"Beer drinkers might disagree with you there, Mom."

Annika leads the way around a small pond, aerating the damp soil with her stilettos. "I don't know why Roger insisted we all walk. This is ridiculous."

"Watch out for cow flops," I say, just to see her flinch.

"Don't be vulgar, Vivien. Especially in front of Lord Tracy."

"Who cares, it's only a title." I can't wait to tour the manor. Visions of gleaming wood and rich silk upholstery are dancing in my head. The building itself is straight out of a fairy tale, sitting in the middle of vast green fields with a forbidding forest behind it. The setting sun casts a golden light over everything. "Will there will be servants, do you think?"

"I would imagine so," Mom says, stepping daintily onto the stile and over the last stone wall. "It's a big house for one person to manage alone."

"Do you think Lord Tracy will be dashing? Lords must be dashing."

"Dashing? No one says *dashing* these days." She stops to scrape mud off her heels with a stick. "You've been reading too many gothic novels. You probably expect Lord Tracy to meet us in a tuxedo."

Actually, I'm picturing something more along the lines of a deep-blue velvet smoking jacket. "As if. A lord would never wear a tuxedo for cocktails."

"Oh, pardon me," she says. But I notice she's perking up ever so slightly.

"Maybe you could marry him and I'll be a princess, almost."

"Or maybe you'll wake up and we'll be back in Kansas, Dorothy."

"Well, you look good tonight," I assure her. "He'd be lucky to get you."

She cracks a half-smile as we start up the tree-lined avenue leading to the main entrance. "Maybe there's already a Lady Tracy."

"If you're nice, he'll dump her for you. But no vulgarity, please."

"I need a drink," she says. But when she turns at the double oak door to fluff my hair and fix my straps, I find she is really smiling. Mission accomplished.

★   ★   ★

We follow the maid through a dark hallway to the parlor, which is much brighter, even though half the bulbs in the chandelier have burned out. The room is crammed with furniture that was probably very fine once, but is shabby now. Worse, there is dog hair on every surface and the wooden feet of the settee and chairs have been chewed. Threadbare carpets are strewn haphazardly over the cracked tile floor.

Lord Tracy has obviously fallen on hard times.

Sean and Roger are already here talking to a pretty young woman in tight tan jodhpurs, black boots, and a crisp white shirt. If that's Lady Tracy, we may be in trouble. Sean excuses himself and hurries over when he sees us; Roger merely nods and turns his full attention to the woman. Damn that Roger. I just boosted Mom's mood into normal range and he knocks it back down with a single nod.

"Howya, Annie," Sean says, giving her a peck on the cheek. He gives me a similar peck, then says, "No time to change out of your wardrobe, kid? Or is this more research?"

Suddenly, my ultrachic dress loses its fabulousness and I'm embarrassed. No one told me it's uncool to pass off my show wardrobe as my own.

Giving me a quick wink, Annika says, "I rushed her and she didn't have time to change. I hate to be late for a party."

I have been repaid for my efforts to cheer her up: the woman just risked a wrinkle to wink at me.

"Well, you do look fantastic," Sean says. "I've borrowed a thing or two from wardrobe in my day." He steers us toward a tarnished silver bar cart that is parked beside Roger and the horsewoman. "Champagne, Annie?"

My mother is too busy eavesdropping on Roger and Miss Horse and Hound to answer. Sean pours her a glass anyway and then offers me a shandy. Unfortunately, Annika picks that moment to regain her hearing. "No shandies tonight," she says firmly.

"Why not?" I ask. "We don't have to work tomorrow."

For a moment, it looks as if she'll relent, but then Miss Horse and Hound lets out a loud laugh and puts her hand on Roger's arm.

"Because I said so," Annika snaps. "End of discussion. Just give her some juice, Sean."

Juice? Why doesn't she insist on a bottle of baby formula and be done with it? Humiliated, I wander over to a scratched coffee table loaded with food. From there, I watch Annika swallow two glasses of champagne in quick succession while keeping an eye on Roger, who is obviously fascinated by the horsewoman. Finally, Annika turns her back to him completely and focuses her attention on Sean, who leads her on a tour of the room. All I see is stuffy old portraits on the wall but Sean must see something more, because he is entertaining my mother to the point where she is tittering like a fool. She'll dislocate her neck if she keeps tossing her head like that.

I consider breaking up their party of two, but something about the way Sean is looking at Annika stops me. It's like he thinks she's the only woman in the room, which she is not. There are nearly fifteen others, including me.

"Would you care for a sherry, young lady?" a soft voice inquires. Turning, I find myself looking into eyes as blue as Sean's. A deeply tanned face and a head of unkempt gray hair make them stand out even more. In the gentleman's right hand is a bottle of sherry; in his left are several tiny glasses. This must be the butler.

"Yes, I would, thanks." I can't help staring at his ratty old suit jacket, stained tie, and scuffed loafers. Lord Tracy obviously isn't paying his staff nearly enough. The butlers in my books are always dressed in patent leather shoes and a crisp uniform.

"You are eighteen, aren't you, lass?"

Eighteen! I knew the dress made me look older but this is more than I dared to hope. "Yes, but maybe I shouldn't—" I begin, my conscience getting the better of me.

But then my mother gives a little squeal. "You're so clever," she tells Sean. Pointing at another portrait, she asks, "And what can you tell me about this dashing young man?"

Dashing? No one says *dashing* these days. "I'd love a glass of sherry," I tell the butler. He pours some into a thimble glass and pours another for himself. I'm a little surprised that Lord Tracy's butler is drinking on the job, but I guess these are more casual times.

"*Sláinte,*" he says, clinking his miniature glass against mine.

"*Sláinte,*" I repeat, taking a sip of the sherry. It's sweet but it burns on the way down and I have to make an effort not to grimace.

"That's a grand dress you're wearing. Reminds me a little of one that my gran wore in her portrait." He points to a full-length painting of a young woman in long blue dress with silver embroidery across the bodice. Although mine shows a lot more skin, the dresses are similar.

"Your gran used to work here, too?" It's great that the family values its staff enough to hang their portraits on the wall.

The butler laughs. "Not exactly, luv. She owned the place." The light is beginning to dawn and I put my hand over my mouth in horror. He bows: "Lord Tracy, at your service." Then he offers me more sherry.

"I am so sorry, sir," I sputter when the burning in my throat stops. "I just assumed since you were serving sherry that you were the butler."

"The peerage isn't what it used to be," he says, laughing even harder. "No one would have mistaken my grandmother for the housekeeper."

"I'm so sorry. I'm from the States. Maybe my manners aren't what they should be."

"Your manners are fine, luv. It's not as if I walk around in a velvet smoking jacket, after all."

"But you're practically royalty."

"Far from it. I'm just an old man with a house and an image I can't afford to maintain."

"You know, my mother is a movie star who *thinks* she's royalty. She says it's a full-time job keeping up appearances."

Lord Tracy smiles as if he finds me entertaining. I do believe the gift of the gab is finally arriving. "That's today's culture of celebrity, I'm afraid. I take it your mother is the lovely woman in red?"

"Yes, how did you know?"

"The apple doesn't fall far from the tree."

"I am *nothing* like my mother," I assure him, watching Annika clutch Sean as if he's a life raft on a stormy sea. "For one thing, I don't flirt with men who are twenty years younger than I am."

"There *are* no men twenty years younger than you are, lass," he says, smiling. "And if you were to ask an old man's opinion, I'd say that the young man is doing most of the flirting."

Finian's arrival gives me an opportunity to study Mom and Sean again. Lord Tracy's eyesight must be failing, because the flirting must be entirely my mother's doing, as it always is. See, she is gazing at Sean and toying with her earring—flirt, flirt, flirt. But why is Sean pushing her hair behind her ear, as if she has lost use of her own hand? And why is his hand on her back as he guides her to another portrait as if she needs his help to navigate?

Just when I think I can't take anymore of the floor show, Mom looks over and sees me standing with Lord Tracy. Sean whispers something in her ear and her face lights up like a theater marquis. Unlike me, Sean knows the difference between a Lord and a butler.

"Leigh, darling!" Annika gushes, dragging Sean to my side. "Aren't you going to introduce us to our gracious host?"

"Lord Tracy, this is Sean Finlay," I say, pretending to ignore my mother until she prods me in the ribs with a pointy fingernail. "Oh, yes, and my mother, Annika Anderson."

"Ms. Anderson, it is a pleasure to make your acquaintance," Lord Tracy says, taking her hand and kissing it. His manners are certainly more polished than his appearance. "Your daughter is absolutely delightful."

"Isn't she just?" Sean says, flinging an arm around my shoulders. With lightning speed, I fling my free arm around his waist. Once it's landed, I rejoice at my own nerve. I've got my arm around Sean Finlay! My hand is actually resting on his hip. If it didn't mean taking my hand away, I would text-message Abby this very instant. My heart is beating so hard that I have to strain to hear my mother's next comment:

"I see she's delighted your Lordship into giving a fifteen-year-old a glass of sherry."

Busted. But how dare she toss my age around like it's nothing to be ashamed of? When will she accept that I am mature beyond my years and deserve to be treated as such? Sean must believe this, because he hasn't moved my arm.

Lord Tracy looks surprised, but is kind enough to cover for me. "Entirely my fault, Ms. Anderson, I'm so sorry. I handed it to her without thinking and she's barely had a sip, have you, lass?"

"I couldn't even taste it you gave me so little, sir. I thought you were just being stingy."

"It hasn't come to that yet, thank god," Lord Tracy says. Fin and Sean both laugh, but my mother is focusing on the arm I have welded to Sean's waist.

I look over at the horsewoman and say, "Do you think we could meet Lady Tracy, sir?"

"There's no Lady Tracy, luv," he says, following my gaze. My mother brightens for a moment, but Fin quickly shakes his head at her. Lord Tracy adds, "That's just a very dear friend and your director is quite welcome to try his luck."

Annika abruptly reaches over and pulls me away from Sean. I almost take his belt with me.

"Thank you so much for your hospitality, Lord Tracy," she says, "but I'm afraid we must go. Bedtime, honey bun."

I will kill her. And then I will bury her in baggy overalls, without any makeup whatsoever.

fourteen

Claiming to be "smothered with a cold," Lucky has taken the day off, leaving us to make our own way into Dublin. I use the fifteen-minute walk to the Bray train station to tell Mom exactly how lame I find her itinerary. She has circled at least a dozen historical sites in the guidebook, claiming that my interest in visiting Blarney Castle inspired her. Now, I'm not against "culture" if it will help flesh out Sinead's character and make me sound worldly back in Seattle, but it obviously needs to be balanced with less intellectual pursuits. Namely, shopping. In the end, I agree not to complain about the "literary tour" of Dublin, as long as she agrees not to complain about my putting some mileage on her credit card during a shopping spree this afternoon. And by the time we board the train, we are both in good moods. Finding the middle ground is something we've rarely accomplished without the help of a tour guide.

I can tell that her list of sites was really a bargaining position anyway. She's wearing a tan suede suit and her usual stilettos. There's no way she expected to hike around ancient ruins all day. My whining was a bargaining strategy, too. I'm actually looking forward to visiting the Dublin Writers Museum, even though the only Irish writer I've studied at school is Oscar Wilde. According to the guidebook, he had a fascinating life—until he got thrown in jail and died penniless and alone. He even had a son named "Vyvyan." I probably wouldn't hate my name so much if it were spelled with *y*'s.

Nah, I still would.

Mom set up a lunch date with Colleen and Finian. Maybe she's as worried about our ability to get through a whole day without killing each other as I am, but at the moment, we're doing okay. In fact, better than okay. We're actually having fun. Since we started rolling toward Dublin, she's been telling stories about her adventures on various film sets, few of which I've heard. Maybe I wasn't interested in showbiz stories before I hung around a set myself, or maybe she was waiting until I was older, since most of the stories involve stars behaving badly. At any rate, she's good storyteller. Her acting seems more polished here on the train than it usually does on set. The only drawback is that her voice is way too loud, as if she were on stage. Sadly, her performance is totally wasted on today's audience, which consists of a handful of commuters who are sound asleep, their heads lolling against the train's windows.

I also notice that Mom favors stories where she looks good and everyone else looks like an idiot. You'd think she never messed up herself. She may look perfect, but if there's one thing I've learned on this trip, it's that she messes up as much as I do. I may have made a fool of myself over Glen Myers, but she's a bigger fool for flirting with Sean when she's old enough to be his mother. Everyone on set is laughing about it.

Everyone except Sean, that is. I can see why he likes her, even apart from her looks. She can be funny if she's in the right mood and she's interesting enough, at least in small doses. What I don't get is why *she* would like him. Oh sure, there's the obvious—he's freakin' gorgeous—but he's about as different from Roger as you can get. I would have thought that "old, rich, and creepy" is her type. That isn't saying much for Dad, I suppose, but they were only together for seven years, whereas Roger seems to have been around longer, on and off. She must be using Sean to annoy Roger.

As much as I hate to risk spoiling our day, I decide to talk to Mom about it. I'm flying home in a few days, so I don't have much time to prove to Sean that I'm the girl for him. She might get in a snit, but it's a sacrifice I'm willing to make.

"Mom, are you interested in Sean?"

"Why this fascination with my love life, darling?" she asks. Cue the fake, tinkling laugh.

"Why this big mystery about your love life?" I say. "You like to talk about mine."

So many people on set knew about Glen Myers dumping me, she must have sent out a bulletin.

"Mine really isn't that interesting—and an actress must avoid boring her audience."

I point to the sleeping passengers around us. "The damage is already done, Mom. Bore away."

"It feels strange to talk about this kind of thing with you," she admits, sighing. "I guess I have to accept that you're growing up."

"That's what I keep telling you."

"Well, then, yes, I do find Sean very sexy." We suddenly plunge into darkness as the train passes through a tunnel. When we emerge, my mother is looking at me. "You don't look well," she says.

"Motion sickness . . . I might throw up." That's what happens when you discover you're doomed. I can't compete with Annika Anderson, even at her advanced age. It's so unfair, when she could get almost any guy in the world.

"I thought you'd be happy if I forgot about Roger."

"But Sean's only twenty-one." My voice sounds strangled.

"Lots of women date younger men these days. It's the latest trend in Hollywood."

"If every other movie star jumped over a cliff, would you?"

Eyeing me curiously, she asks, "Why does this bother you so much?"

How can the woman not know, when everyone else on set—

including Sean and Roger—has figured it out? If she had the slightest bit of maternal insight, she'd be able to see how I feel. "Because it's embarrassing. Everyone will talk about it."

"I embarrass you all the time anyway. If you think I don't know what you're telling your friend Abby in those messages, think again."

Okay, so give her one point for maternal insight. "I just think Sean would be better off with someone younger." Turning, I cough into my hand, *"Like me."*

"What?" Her eyes are wide with surprise.

It's now or never: "I happen to be in love with him, if you must know." There, I said it. Now she'll have to give up Sean since she knows how serious I am. It's the kind of sacrifice any mother would make for her kid.

"In love with him? That's impossible, you're only fifteen!" Her voice wakes the guy two rows ahead.

"In Oscar Wilde's day, girls were already married at my age."

"In Oscar Wilde's day, men were thrown in jail for falling love with other men. I don't imagine you want to return to that era."

"Oh Mother." I throw myself back in my seat and stare at the ceiling of the train.

"Sean is too old for you."

"He's only six years older than me—and twenty years younger than you."

She instantly gets that pinched look she always wears when the subject of her age comes up. "I see you've got a firm grasp of numbers. I'm glad we're not just throwing our money away on that Academy."

Now that the gloves are off, I feel free to throw her own words at her. "In 'Hollywood years,' you're actually *forty* years older than Sean."

"Make your next film a comedy, you're hilarious." Opening her purse, she takes out her compact and inspects her makeup. Finally she closes it, saying, "Sean hasn't asked you out, has he?"

"Not exactly."

"What does that mean?"

I consider lying, but she'd just ask him herself on Monday and humiliate me more. "Maybe he *would* if you weren't laughing too hard at his jokes and cooing over his crappy flowers."

"I don't!"

"You do," I insist. "I know you're just trying to make Roger jealous, but Sean won't give me a chance because of you. It's so unfair, because you're just using him whereas I really care about him."

We're quiet for several minutes—long enough for the guy two rows ahead to fall asleep again. And when she finally speaks, it's in a kinder voice. "Leigh, believe it or not, the gap between fifteen and twenty-one is greater than it is between twenty-one and forty-one."

I snort.

"Look," she continues, "the film is almost over and we'll all go back to our real lives soon. Most on-set connections never survive that transition."

"Then why bother going out with Sean if it's going nowhere?"

Shrugging, she says, "How about neither of us goes out with Sean?"

"But *I'm* perfect for him. If he asks me, how could I say no?"

"Try this: *give me a call in four years.*"

"Four years! That's forever."

"You just reminded me how time flies in Hollywood years. If you still want to go out with him then, I won't stand in your way."

"Just promise me you won't make him my stepfather in the meantime."

She laughs and pats my arm. "That I can promise."

Relaxing, I suggest, "Or maybe we could do a reality show about a mother who marries the love of her daughter's life. I don't think it's been done."

"There's a reason for that, darling: poor taste."

That's usually a plus on reality television, from what I can tell.

★ ★ ★

Mom rotates the map ninety degrees and tilts her head with it. "I think we're nearly there." For the past two hours, she's been struggling with the guide for the literary walking tour of Dublin. I'm sure we've been down this street before.

"Great, I can't wait to see another crumbling old house."

"George Bernard Shaw is a legend. I would give anything to star in one of his plays."

"I would give anything to sit down. Aren't your feet killing you?"

"I told you, I was born in these things."

Finally, we reach Thirty Synge Avenue, an old auto body shop wedged between several houses. I peer over Mom's shoulder as she checks her book again. "Shaw's birthplace is number Thirty Synge Street and we're on Synge Avenue," I say, pointing at the street sign.

That's when we notice the drumming. As we stand listening, it gets louder and louder and the beat is so mesmerizing that I forget all about my aching feet and start walking toward the sound. The streets eventually open up into Meeting House Square, where we see dozens of drummers on a stage, each with a bodhran under his arm. Colleen told me about these ancient Irish goatskin drums. She failed to mention that most drummers are attractive young men, however, or I'd have checked out a performance weeks ago.

Mom must agree that they're pretty sexy, because she smiles and nods when I suggest taking a load off her stilettos. In fact, we sit through two sets and she doesn't make a move to go until Colleen finally calls from her cell phone to find out why we're late for lunch.

★ ★ ★

I wanted to eat at the Clarence Hotel, which is owned by U2, but Mom refused. She's already met Bono at L.A. fund-raisers, she said, and she wasn't impressed. "He's always rambling on about changing the world. It's so boring." Besides, she adds, La Caprice has a far better view. La Caprice does indeed have a better view—of her. There are mirrors everywhere. And before we've even taken our seats, Jeannie Stringer, the star of Ireland's most popular sit-com, hurries over. She and Mom worked together on some schlocky movie of the week years ago and became the best of friends— although they haven't actually spoken since.

"Jeannie," my mother says, using her loud, stage voice, "this is my daughter Vivien."

Wow, we have made some progress in a month if she's willing to admit our real relationship to a celebrity. "Spelled with two y's," I tell Jeannie, "but you can call me Leigh."

"She has her father's sense of humor," Mom explains, giving me a vicious little pinch.

"Don't apologize," Jeannie reassures her, "I have kids too."

That's when mom really surprises me: "You know, Jeannie," she says, "Roger gave Vivien Leigh a role in *Danny Boy* and she's doing quite well."

"Really?" Jeannie looks at me as if I'm suddenly of more interest. "She's obviously a chip off the old block."

Finian's arrival stops me from commenting on how old the block really is. He practically takes flight when he sees Jeannie. She, in turn, hurls herself into his outstretched arms. Their screaming is deafening. I don't find the attention we're getting from the other diners as rewarding as I expected.

After an animated discussion, Finian finally walks Jeannie to the door and returns to sit opposite to Mom. "I think she's had her eyes done," he whispers.

"Fin!" Mom is horrified. "What are you saying about *me* to other stars?"

"That you've had your lips done, Baby Doll."

She puts her hand over her mouth and glares at him.

"Don't worry, Mom, they're already half the size they were when I got here."

."Where's Colleen?" Mom asks from behind her hand. "I need someone on my side."

"I'm always on your side," Fin says, taking her hand. "At least until Leigh gets first billing."

Mom orders her usual restaurant fare: a salad with grilled chicken, dressing on the side. Fin, Colleen, and I order burgers and fries. While we're waiting for our food, I happen to glance toward the door and see a familiar face—a face that sets off a bodhran drum solo in my chest. Discovering my own stage voice, I say, "It's Sean."

Colleen and Fin turn quickly to look, but the guy has already stepped out the door. Fin says, "Wishful thinking, Leigh."

"It was him. He's worn that blue shirt on set."

My mother has continued to cut her greens into tiny bites, as if this were a nonevent. "Don't encourage her, Fin. We've had this discussion today already."

Giving my arm a sympathetic squeeze, Colleen says, "Don't fret. In my experience, a plate of chips cures all."

"And you wonder why you're still single," Fin says.

"Shut yer gob, Finian Doyle," Colleen says, pretending to stab him with her fork.

There's so much chatter over the next hour that it takes me a while to notice that Mom has faded out of the conversation. She's pushing her salad around with her fork and it doesn't look like she's eaten a bit of it. "What's wrong, Mom?" I ask.

"Nothing, darling, I'm just tired. In fact, I was thinking I might leave you three for a bit this afternoon and have a massage. Shopping is *so* exhausting. Would you mind?"

Of course I mind. We're supposed to be spending the day together and now she's ditching me at the first chance. But I won't give her the satisfaction of seeing that it bothers me. "Go for it. Colleen and Fin and I can hit some pubs."

Taking a credit card from her purse, she hands it to me. "*Shopping,* I said, not a pub crawl."

"Ooh-hoo. Where do they sell Rock and Republic jeans, Colleen?" I ask. "Do you want a pair, too?"

Mom tries to snatch the card back, but Colleen is too fast for her. "I'm partial to Earl jeans, myself," she says, slipping the card into her pocket. "Consider it the price of my personal shopping guide services, Annika. Just be grateful that Fin doesn't wear anything under that caftan."

"A set of day-of-the-week thongs might be nice," he says.

We're still groaning when the waiter drops the check in front of Mom.

★ ★ ★

Three hours later, Colleen juggles several shopping bags to reach for her cell phone. It's my mother, calling from the spa. They speak for a few minutes, before Colleen says, "Sure, no problem, but it'll cost you a pair of shoes."

"She's not coming back, is she?" I ask, as she hangs up.

"Now that she's there, she wants the full deal—manicure, pedicure, facial. She'll be so late she suggested we head back to Bray without her."

"Oh come on, Colleen, no spa stays open that late. She's meeting up with Roger."

Exchanging glances with Finian, Colleen says, "I don't know about *that,* but don't let it ruin your day, anyway. We can do anything you want."

"Then I want to get a tattoo."

"Not on our watch," Finian says. "We're returning you in the state we found you."

Instead, we shop some more. I stock up on Stila lip gloss and Hard Candy sonic sparkle dust. Because I'm mad at my mother, I also pick up a low-slung miniskirt that I know Dad will never let me wear. If she were really going to a spa, she'd have said so earlier. Mom's never been shy about putting herself first. She's just afraid to tell me she's running back into Roger's arms, because she knows I won't approve. Meanwhile, I'll be gone soon and she won't see me for months, if not years.

I feel better after buying some Juicy sweatpants and a hoodie. I choose another set as a gift for Abby and charge those to Mom's card, too. Surprisingly, Colleen and Fin encourage me.

"She can afford it," Colleen says. "Here, take one of these Celtic design necklaces."

"What about this?" I ask, pointing to a silver ring that features a tiny pair of hands holding a heart topped with a crown.

"That's the Claddagh ring," she says, going on to explain the meaning behind it. The heart symbolizes inner tenderness, the hands symbolize the intimacy between the giver and receiver, and the crown is for the protection of the heart. If the ring is a gift from a husband or boyfriend, you wear it on your left hand, with the heart pointed toward your heart to let the world know that you're taken. But you can also wear it on your right hand with the heart pointed away from you as a symbol of love and friendship, which can signal that you're single and looking.

Finian winks at me. "It's the only way Colleen has ever worn hers."

Colleen punches him hard in the arm.

Someday maybe Sean will slip a Claddagh ring onto my left hand. In the meantime, I buy one for Abby.

★ ★ ★

Fin stops in front of the Irish film center and points at a poster for *Gone with the Wind*. He's shocked to hear that I've never seen the movie before. "Well, it starts in fifteen minutes, so this must be fate."

"I hate my name, why would I want to see the movie that inspired it?"

"Because it's a fantastic film and Vivien Leigh is magical in it."

He propels Colleen and me toward the ticket line. "That's why they call it a classic."

The movie's corny dialogue is embarrassing at first. "This is totally lame," I whisper to Finian. "When does the car chase start?" Soon, however, I'm caught up in the story in spite of myself. A spoiled socialite, Scarlett O'Hara's heroic nature only emerges as tragedy overtakes her life. By the time the credits roll, she has survived a civil war, the death of her parents, the loss of her beloved home, and heartbreak over lost love. Still, she is strong and determined. When the lights finally come up, tears are streaming down my face. "Okay, so it wasn't bad," I say, sheepishly mopping my face with my sleeve, "but it could have used some special effects."

"An entire state burns. That isn't enough for you?"

"It needed an action sequence, where Scarlett pulls up her hoop skirt and delivers some Kung Fu kicks to those Yankee soldiers."

Fin is still shaking his head as he leaves us and heads up the street. "Don't expect me to do your hair on any superhero movies, Baby Doll. A sad waste of my talent—and yours."

★　★　★

Colleen and I stroll toward the train station arm in arm. I think the best part of my trip to Ireland has been getting to know Fin and Colleen. It's the first time I've had friends who aren't my own age.

"So," Colleen says, "is *Danny Boy* just a summer fling or are you going to do some acting back in Seattle?"

"I don't know, I haven't thought about it," I say. Which is a lie, because I have thought about it. A lot.

"Why don't you take some classes? Fin and I think you're really good."

"Yeah, but you like me."

"Not that much. We're just putting up with you to get into Annie's wallet." She holds up the bag with her new jeans.

"Hey," I say, sighting the sign for the Clarence Hotel. "That's the place U2 owns. Can we walk past it?"

We're still nearly half a block away when I see them: a blond woman in a tan suede suit and a dark-haired man in a blue shirt. They're walking toward the hotel entrance. Colleen sees them at the same time and grabs my arm. I try to pull away from her to chase after them, but she holds me back. Meanwhile the man slides his arm around the woman's narrow shoulders and guides her up the hotel walk and into the hotel. Standing there, my arm hanging limply from Colleen's hand, I feel as though there's a wind blowing right through my head.

"Don't faint on me now," Colleen says, leading me to a bench. She pushes me down and sits beside me.

"I can't believe it," I whisper. "She's having a fling with Sean."

"She's *going into a hotel* with Sean. A hotel with a very nice restaurant. They're eating together—it's no big deal."

"My mother doesn't eat," I say.

"So they're having a drink then."

"I told her this morning how I feel about him and she said she wouldn't see him."

"What did she say, exactly?"

I think about it for a moment. "I said, 'promise me you won't make him my stepfather,' and she did."

Sighing, Colleen says, "There's a lot of room between 'dating' and 'stepparenting.'"

Something in her tone makes me ask, "Did you know she was seeing him, Colleen?"

She shakes her head. "I knew Sean fancied her and I knew she was trying to get over Roger. I was afraid if he caught her at a weak moment, she might give in."

"How could she, when she knows how I feel?"

"Your mother's self-esteem has taken a beating lately. She's just trying to feel better about herself."

"She's always thinking about herself. I should never have trusted her." I stand and start walking quickly up the street, away from the hotel. Colleen, left with all the shopping bags, struggles to collect them and hurries after me.

"Give her a chance to explain."

"She's all out of chances."

Colleen is obviously on Mom's side, so I barely speak to her during the train ride home. I make a point of being polite, of thanking her for spending the day with me, but I won't talk anymore about Mom. And since that's the only thing either of us can think about at the moment, there really isn't much to say anyway.

★ ★ ★

My hand is shaking so much I have to try the number three times.

"Why, it's after midnight there, dear," Grandma says when she hears my voice. "You should be in bed. Where's your mother?"

I can't tell her that Annika is at a hotel with a twenty-one-year-old actor. If there's the slightest chance that she hasn't totally betrayed me, the last person I can share the story with is Grandma. I wouldn't put it past her to climb on a plane and arrive in Bray by sunrise. "She's asleep," I say. "Is Millie with you?"

"She's in the next room watching Percival."

"Watching Percival do what?"

"Sleep. She sits by his chair for hours, waiting for him to open his eyes. Percy is actually giving that dog a second chance, if you can believe it, and they may end up friends yet."

"Grandma, how many chances do you give *people*?"

"Well, it depends on the situation. I've given Stan a few. But remember the old saying: Fool me once, shame on you, fool me twice, shame on me. Are we talking about your mother?"

"No, I'm just thinking about stuff."

"Well don't sit up too long thinking. Everything looks better in the morning."

★　★　★

I'm curled on my side watching the bedroom door when Annika finally creeps into the kitchen. The crack of light under the door hits
the clock: 3:23 A.M. She must have taken a cab, because the trains
stopped long ago.

Tiptoeing into the bedroom, Mom slides out of her clothes almost soundlessly. She must be desperate not to wake me, because
she breaks her own cardinal rule about going to bed without wash-
ing off her makeup. "Treat your face like the finest china," she always says. I've pointed out that fine china doesn't require thousands
of dollars worth of products or a cosmetic surgeon on speed dial,
but she says her face is her living and worth every penny she
spends. Tonight she risks her living to sneak into bed. She pulls the
covers up and sighs, sending a gust of boozy fumes my way.

Good. She should sleep very soundly as I plot my revenge.

fifteen

In the faint gray light of dawn, the traitor slumbers on. I, on the other hand, have been awake the entire night, listening to her deep, even breaths and hoping that her conscience won't kick in until after the alarm rings at 8:00 A.M. By that time, I'll be sipping hot chocolate at Bewley's Café on Grafton Street.

Creeping out of bed I fumble for a T-shirt and my new jeans, and grab the knapsack I tucked under the cot last night. It contains everything I'll need to survive awhile in Dublin: three novels (two of which Sean lent me before Annika stole him), socks and undies, the Juicy hoodie, a "Kiss Me I'm Irish" T-shirt, my bulging makeup bag, and a cheese sandwich on soda bread. I even threw in my plane ticket and passport, just in case. Maybe I'll move up my flight and make my mother ship the rest of my stuff after me. Her toy boy can carry my suitcase so that she doesn't break a nail.

In the kitchen, I slip into my clothes and spread the Dart schedule on the table to confirm that the first train leaves Bray for Dublin at 6:00 A.M. I tiptoe out the door, close it carefully behind me, and creep down the porch stairs. My breath is coming in short, nervous gasps. If I can just get through the front gate without being caught, I should be fine. I look back as I reach it and there's no sign of life.

The rain that hammered the cottage roof all night has slowed to a drizzle. I tramp up the narrow lane toward the station, my sneakers making a rhythmic squelch on the gravel. One of Mrs. O'Reilly's corny folk songs pops into my head and I sing the last line out loud:

Ah, the cares of tomorrow can wait till this day is done.

As I near the main cottage, a sudden rustle in the hedgerow stops me. I listen for a moment, but hear only the patter of rain on leaves. My imagination must be working overtime. When I start walking, however, I hear it again. I could swear I am being followed, but no human being could crouch and run behind that hedgerow for long. Maybe it's some deranged Freddy Kruger–like leprechaun? Picking up the pace, I jog up the lane. No matter how fast I go the rustling stays just behind me. Panicking, I break into a full-out run toward the shadowy form of Mrs. O'Reilly's cottage.

At her gate, I slow to a stop and listen: the rustling has stopped. I strain to hear above the pounding of my own heart, but whatever it was, it's gone, leaving me drenched in sweat in the chill morning breeze. Leaning on the stone wall to catch my breath, I watch the sun stretching long rays over the horizon. The light is reassuring and my heart rate slows.

But then, as I turn to continue on my way, a dirty, wet, black-and-white bomb explodes in my face.

"Woof!"

Skip knocks me to the ground and covers me with sloppy kisses. There is no more dangerous a beast than a bored sheepdog without a flock. Having ruthlessly stalked and ambushed me, he is now bragging about it with a volley of triumphant barks. If I don't shut him up fast, Mrs. O will heave herself out of bed, shuffle to the door, and find me lying almost at her feet. Then I'll have some explaining to do.

The hand signals I used on Skip before just make him bark harder today. I move on to plan B. Reaching into my backpack, I grab the cheese sandwich and offer it to the dog, just as a light flicks on in the cottage. When I scramble to my feet and bolt, Skip doesn't even look up from his sandwich. Soon he's just a fuzzy dot in the distance.

I keep running. Despite my sleepless night, I feel a surge of energy. The air is crisp and salty and my sneakers seem to be full of springs. If I knew running felt this good, I'd have tried out for track long ago. Not that the Academy encourages athletics, mind you. If you want to learn how to program a computer, build robots, or play cyber-chess, there are loads of clubs to choose from, but most years we can't even get a track team together. It's a miracle I'm not a total nerd.

At the Irish International Bank, I use my Interac card to withdraw 100 euro dollars from the bank account that I opened for my *Danny Boy* wages. It seems like a lot of money, but I have to buy a train ticket and I'll need food and maybe even a place to stay in Dublin. Also, to celebrate my freedom, I'm finally going to get that tattoo. Scarring myself for life is probably the most offensive thing I could do to punish Annika.

I reach the train station with ten minutes to spare before the first commuter into Connolly Station.

"A one-way ticket to Dublin, please," I tell the man in the booth. What do I have to go back to? Besides, one-way is cheaper.

"Sixteen Euros."

Yikes! My cash isn't going to stretch as far as I hoped.

Boarding the train, I choose a seat opposite a motherly looking lady who is dozing against the window. She awakens as the train pulls out of the station and offers me a buttered scone. I accept it gratefully and we chew in silence as the green fields fly past. For the moment, my nervousness has disappeared. All I feel is excitement: I am alone in the world! Independent! A free agent!

If Dad could see me now, he'd flip.

Settling back into my seat, I imagine the reaction when Mom discovers I'm gone.

Scene 32: They'll Be Sorry

Cottage bedroom, early morning.

Annika is lying on her back, yesterday's makeup smeared across her face. A stream of spittle runs from the side of her mouth down her cheek to pool on the pillow. In the distance, a dog barks repeatedly. We hear someone call to the dog and the barking gets louder until the door bursts open. Mrs. O'Reilly steps into the room, her sheepdog Skip at her heels.

> MRS. O
> Rise and shine, you two! Lucky will be
> here in a few minutes.

She draws back the thick lace curtains and Annika groans as harsh sunlight floods the room. Walking over to the cot, Mrs. O'Reilly flings back the covers only to find two pillows arranged vertically, topped by a stuffed brown dog meant to pass for mousy hair. Beside the pillows is the body of a Madame Alexander Greta Garbo doll with its head ripped off.

> MRS. O
> Where's the gersha?

Annika yawns and turns her head slightly to look at the cot.

> ANNIKA
> She must have gone for a walk.

MRS. O

It's raining. She hates rain.

ANNIKA

I'm sure she's just walked to the studio on
her own.

MRS. O

She'd have left a note. Did you see this
thing?

Mrs. O holds up the headless doll for Annika's inspec-
tion.

MRS. O

She may be in trouble.

ANNIKA

That's just her strange sense of humor.
She's fine, don't worry. You know, I'm starv-
ing today, for some reason. How about a
fry-up?

MRS. O

Get up and get dressed. We're going to find
your daughter.

Annika stares into space, seemingly unconcerned. Mrs. O
casually flicks a finger at Skip, who rushes to the bed
and barks incessantly at Annika until she gets up.
Then he pushes against her legs, forcing her into the
bathroom. The dog then notices something poking out
from under the cot: a strand of blond curly hair.

*Retrieving the head of Greta, he settles outside the
bathroom door for a chew.*

*Outside, Lucky is waiting in the idling Audi. Clutching
her bathrobe to her throat, Mrs. O'Reilly hurries out
of the cottage and gets into the front seat of the car.*

LUCKY

What's wrong?

MRS. O

The gersha's gone. Her ma thinks she walked
to rehearsal, but I don't believe it. I can't
rest until I make sure she's all right.

LUCKY

Will Her Highness be joining us?

MRS. O

She'll be right out.

*Annika saunters down the path to the car. She has ob-
viously put careful thought into the demands of her
new role as "concerned mother." Her hair is in an elaborate updo and she's wearing a sober, dark suit. There
may be photo ops, after all.*

*The Audi streaks across the Irish countryside toward
the military base that serves as the studio. Mrs. O
leaps out before the car has completely stopped and
races into the building. No one in the history of
mankind has ever made better time in a housecoat.*

Annika, however, pauses at the craft services truck in the parking lot to pick up a cappuccino. She lights a cigarette and studies the sunrise before finally making an effort to catch up with Mrs. O'Reilly.

Mrs. O is standing beside Annika's trailer.

> MRS. O
> She's nowhere to be found. I'm sure the poor girl has run away. [Accusingly] What did you do?

> ANNIKA
> What does this have to do with *me?*

Mrs. O takes a menacing step toward Annika.

> ANNIKA
> [backing away]
> Well, maybe she found out that I'm seeing Sean.

> MRS. O
> [shocked]
> Sean! The boy she fancies?

> ANNIKA
> He's not a boy, he's a man—and far too old for her. He'd never be interested in a child, so why should I give up a chance for a little fun?

MRS. O

Because you're her *mother*? I'm calling her
da to see if he's heard from her.

*Snatching Annika's cell phone, she dials the number
posted on the trailer wall. After informing Leigh's father about what's happened, she passes the phone to Annika. His yelling can be heard across the room.*

ANNIKA

Oh Dennis, lighten up. She's fine. She's just
trying to get my attention. The girl's a
bit of a drama queen, you know.

MRS. O
[rolling her eyes]
I wonder where she gets that from?

*As Roger appears at the trailer door, Annika hangs up
the phone without even saying good-bye. Her enormous
eyes promptly fill with tears.*

ANNIKA

Roger, my baby ran away in the night! I've
been absolutely frantic with worry!

MRS. O

That's a load of old cobbler. The girl
could be dead in an alley, yet you still
took the time to do your makeup.

*Roger shoots Annika a look of disgust before summon-
ing Colleen, who confirms that Leigh has not arrived.*

ROGER
[urgently]
Colleen, call the police. She could be in
trouble and I can't risk losing my Sinead.
Leigh was perfect in the role. *Perfect!* We
must find her immediately.

*Behind him, Annika is pouting. There is only one per-
fect actress in this production and it isn't Leigh Reid.
And hearing Roger finally get the kid's name right
twists the knife even deeper.*

ANNIKA
Her real name is Vivien, you know. Make
sure you tell *that* to the police.

*Colleen calls the police on her cell phone, then rushes
off to warn Sean, Finian, Mary, and Maude. Meanwhile,
Annika puts her hand to her forehead and drops onto
the trailer's couch.*

ANNIKA
Roger, I'm faint. Could you get me a glass
of water?

ROGER
[walking out the door]
Get it yourself.

*Annika pouts as the others gather outside the trailer
door.*

COLLEEN
I'm afraid this might have something to
do with what happened yesterday.

ANNIKA
[standing in the doorway]
What do you mean?

COLLEEN
Leigh and I saw you and Sean going into
the Clarence Hotel together last night.

*Annika's face turns bright red and she clutches the
doorframe for support. Roger turns to her and scowls before barking instructions to the small search party.*

ROGER
Colleen, you check out the places in
Dublin you visited with Leigh yesterday.
The rest of you start combing the country-
side in your cars. I want that girl found.

ANNIKA
People, you're overreacting. This is a
shameless ploy to attract attention and
you're playing right into her hands! She'll
come home when she gets hungry.

*There's a collective gasp. Roger is the first to find his
tongue.*

ROGER

You have less maternal feeling than an iguana.

COLLEEN

It's horrible!

MRS. O

It's heartless!

FINIAN

It's hideous!

MARY AND MAUDE
[in unison]

It's inhuman!

Then the search party fans out, with Mrs. O'Reilly bringing up the rear, her housecoat flapping as she runs. She turns and shouts a string of curses over her shoulder until we can no longer hear her.

MRS. O

May your teeth yellow and rot!
May your body grow soft and large!
May your hair no longer curl!
May your lips lose their color!
May the world see your true face!

Sean and Annika are alone in the trailer. He looks at her sadly.

                            SEAN
Why would Leigh do this, Annie? Did you
have an argument?

                           ANNIKA
You heard Colleen. Leigh saw us together
in Dublin yesterday.

                            SEAN
So?

                           ANNIKA
          [selling out her daughter completely]
The little fool thinks she's in love with
you. It would be sweet if it weren't so ab-
surd.

                            SEAN
             [suddenly starry-eyed]
In love? With me?

                           ANNIKA
Don't pretend you didn't notice.

                            SEAN
I never thought she'd be serious about a
wanker like me. I'm not good enough for
her.

                           ANNIKA
                        [bristling]
But you're good enough for *me*?

SEAN

Come on, now, Annie. You're all right for a
bit of fun, but, Leigh, she's *GM*.

ANNIKA

GM?

SEAN

Girlfriend material. I've got to find her
before it's too late!

ANNIKA
[outraged]
Let the others find her. You stay here
with me!

SEAN

Oh, grow up, Annie. We had a few laughs,
but my beloved Leigh is·missing and I
must be the one to find her.

ANNIKA

Don't you dare leave me!

SEAN
[as he runs off set]
By the way, have you gained weight?

Annika gasps in horror and looks down at her stomach,
which is indeed expanding by the minute. Mrs. O's curses
are already taking effect.

*Sitting alone in her trailer, Annika is forced to undo
the zipper of her now-too-tight pants. She sobs as her
hair returns to its natural mousy brown and her lus-
trous curls grow limp and lank. Her skin becomes pock-
marked and her lips, now withered and pale, hang
slackly over crooked, cappuccino-stained teeth. As we
fade out, she is trying in vain to apply Glazed Poppy
lipstick, but it won't adhere.*

"Connolly Station!" the ticket collector bellows, startling me
out of my daydream. "You were a million miles away, love," he says
as I pass him to exit the train.

"I was just thinking," I say. "I have a lot on my mind."

"Well, whatever it was, you were enjoying it. There was a smile
a mile wide on your face."

sixteen

I practically skip across the Ha'penny Bridge, because the rain has finally stopped and everything is going as planned. At least it is until I reach Bewley's Café on Grafton Street, which isn't supposed to be closed. It's 7:15, what gives? Disappointed, I pick up a large cup of tea at a greasy spoon, instead. Whatever else Ireland has done for me, it's given me an unexpected appreciation for the national beverage. I like the chips, too.

I soon find myself on a bench at Trinity College, watching groggy-looking students drag themselves to class. In just two years, that will be me. I have always imagined that the books under my arms will cover common diseases of the parakeet, but lately, a question keeps rolling around in my brain: Why not become an actress? Not a second-rate movie-of-the-week actress like Annika Anderson, but a *real* actress, like Charlize Theron or Gwyneth Paltrow.

Part of me hopes this acting thing is a passing phase. I've spent my whole life thinking it's a crock and who could blame me, with Mom's crappy movies as my example? I never understood the big draw. Yet, here I am, thinking about abandoning my dream of saving animal lives because of one tiny role in a movie. There's obviously something addictive about the film business.

Not that it's easy. I took the role of Sinead to be closer to Sean, but it's turned out to be really challenging. Pretending to be someone else in front of a camera is much harder than pulling off an A in Al-gebra class. What's more, Roger's rare bits of praise have given me more of a buzz than earning an A ever did.

"It's all about discipline," Roger says. "There are no shortcuts."

Well, I can be disciplined. I'm reasonably smart. And I have a good memory. If acting can be taught, I can learn it. If it's an inborn gift, on the other hand, I'm in big trouble unless Annika turns out not to be my real mother after all.

Okay, she's not awful. Well, some days she is awful, but most days, when she's not freaking out about Roger or about being old and ugly, she's not half-bad. I may hate her, but I can see that she has some acting ability. If she got her life straightened out, she might do better. Since I book her schedule, I can see that she doesn't have a lot of friends and she's proven that she gets hung up on the wrong guys. She must be lonely.

Not that it's any excuse for her stealing *my* guy.

I'm still mulling over my mother's empty life when a girl sits down beside me. She's obviously a student, although she doesn't look that much older than me. Pulling the tab back on her coffee cup, she says, "Howya."

"Howya," I reply.

"Can you believe this load of books?" she asks, setting the stack on the bench between us. "I'm keeping the chiropractor in busi-ness." Noticing my overstuffed knapsack, she continues, "You must be here for student orientation."

"So I am," I say, slipping smoothly into Sinead's Dublin accent. Time to see if my acting skills are worth anything.

"You're local, then?"

I nod, thrilled that I'm pulling it off with an Irish native. "What are you studying?"

"Everything and nothing, I'm afraid. I started out in the arts, but my astronomy course is so deadly that I may switch to science. How about you?"

"I was planning to be a vet, but lately I'm not so sure."

"Just wait, you'll discover courses you never knew existed. It's mad!"

We chat for a while longer, but too soon, the girl stands to leave. As she gathers her things, she turns over my book, *Angela's Ashes*. "That one's a heartbreaker, isn't it? If you're a reader, you should visit the *Book of Kells*. It's twelve hundred years old—one of the most famous books in the world." She points to a section of the university behind me. "It's just across the way in the library."

"Thanks, I will."

Scribbling something on a slip of paper, she says, "I know what it's like to be the new girl on campus, so why don't you ring me when you've settled in? I'll show you the best places to find cute guys."

I accept the slip of paper happily. I may not be so good at making new friends at home, but I'm doing all right in Ireland.

I've probably been too mature for high school all along.

Since my new friend Siobhan recommends it, I join the queue to see the *Book of Kells* once the library opens. Any book that's survived this long is worth a look, I guess, but the blurb on the wall says it contains the four gospels in Latin. Bor-ing. How could it take monks in an island monastery thirty years to complete? The answer becomes clear when I get closer: the pages are filled with intricate Celtic designs, featuring vines and animals and flowers. Each is like a beautiful stained-glass window, the colors still bright.

I buy an illustrated booklet about the *Book of Kells* from the souvenir shop and return to my bench to read until the sky clouds over again and fat raindrops splatter on the pages.

★　★　★

My first big mistake was leaving my mother's credit card on the kitchen table in Bray. I did it intentionally, to make the point that I don't need her. Although it's a very good point, I realize now that

I could have made it differently. It means I have to settle for window-shopping today.

Not that it stops me from trying on half a dozen outfits at Envy, in the St. Stephen's Green Shopping center. Just in case I still make it to the *Danny Boy* wrap party.

I'm eating chips in the food court when I notice the sign: Celestial Ring Tattoos. Finally it all comes together: I have the cash, I have the venue, I have the freedom. Now all I need is a decision on what and where. Out of respect for (make that "fear of") Grandma Reid, it will have to be small and easily hidden. This rules out the arms and legs and basically leaves my stomach and back. I liked the tiny fairy Abby's cousin had at the base of her spine; it's the perfect size and the perfect location. I'll go with that.

A sign on the door says Celestial Ring will not tattoo anyone under the age of eighteen. That's very bad news for Leigh Reid. Sinead O'Leary, however, just passed for college-age on campus.

The woman at the gleaming counter has half a dozen African animals tattooed on her arms, two rings over one eyebrow, and another ten running up one ear. She watches me flip through the catalog of designs with a suspicious expression on her face. "Can I help you?" she asks. She's not much over twenty herself, so who is she to sound all teacherish?

"Not yet, thanks," I say, in my best Sinead accent. Trying to get a little repartee going, I add, "These are deadly tats. Are you the artist?"

"I am," she says. "How can I help you?" Scamming this woman is likely going to take some fancy footwork on Sinead's part, but it will help me stretch as an actress.

"I'm just trying to settle on a design," I say, as if it's already a done deal. "Do you have any images from the *Book of Kells*?" Surely my knowledge of one of the oldest books in the world will make me seem worldly and mature.

"I might," she says, sounding unimpressed. "Do you have any ID?"

"ID?" I repeat, stalling for time.

"I-den-ti-fi-ca-tion."

She pronounces the syllables slowly, as if I were an imbecile. I resist the urge to enlighten her about the Academy. For the moment, Sinead wants a tattoo more than revenge.

"Fine, what kind do you need?" I make a show of rifling through my knapsack.

"The kind that proves you're eighteen."

"Oh, *that* kind!" I allow myself a hint of sarcasm. "Well, the photo on my driver's license is so desperate that I don't show it until I have to. Let me settle on a design first." I try to smile sweetly, but it feels more like a scowl.

"Look, kid," she says, pulling the catalog out of my hands so fast I lurch forward, "I run a respectable business here and I don't tattoo anyone under the age of eighteen without parental permission. Since I don't see a parent here, I'll have to ask you to leave."

"My parents are totally onside with the whole body art thing. Who do you think gave me the cash to have the work done?" Playing my last card, I display the stack of euros in my wallet. Maybe if she sees the money, she'll make an exception. In fact, maybe she'll take a bribe.

"Save your money for the zoo, kid. I'm not giving you a tattoo."

"Well, thanks for nothing," I snap, turning to leave.

"You're welcome," she says, with a nasty little smile. There's a ruby chip in her front tooth.

Fine. I wouldn't want a smart-ass like her doing my ink anyway. If I asked for a Celtic cross on my back, she'd probably do a big ugly iguana just to spite me. I'd either end up spending my *Danny Boy* earnings to laser it off or I'd never show my back again, which kind of defeats the purpose.

My point is, getting a tattoo is serious business. You have to be able to trust your artist.

★   ★   ★

At the stationery store on Grafton Street, I buy a purple notepad
and write:

> To Whom it May Concern,
> Please accept this note as permission for my
> daughter, Leigh Reid, age eighteen, to get a tattoo.
> I defer to Leigh's superior judgment about the size,
> type, and location of said tattoo.
>   Sincerely,
>   Annika Anderson

There's more than one tattoo parlor in Dublin, and next time,
I'll be prepared. After rereading my letter, I add "actress" after Annika's name. If the locals keep up with the celebrity gossip, they're
bound to know about *Danny Boy*. And if they haven't seen any of
her films, they might just be impressed.

★   ★   ★

The kid with the dragon tattoo at the corner store directed me to a
place called Life Art on a nearby side street, but I have to walk the
length of the block three times before I finally see a flashing sign in
a second-floor window. A couple of lights have been removed from
the sign and it reads: "FART." Nice.

Determined not to be put off by the peeling paint on the walls, I
follow the loud punk music up the stairs, to the door marked Life
Art. It opens on a small reception area, where a ratty orange blanket
partially covers an even rattier sofa. A broken disco ball hangs over
the counter, behind which a shaved head bobs violently to the music.

Leigh would have left at a dead run; fortunately Sinead is an
adventurer.

The Head doesn't even look up as I approach the counter to
scan the tattoo designs displayed on the wall. Nothing resembles the

illustrations in the *Book of Kells,* and the fairies all have grotesque expressions on their faces, but there's an interesting four-leaf clover. It's no bigger than my thumbnail and in its center is a tiny, purple heart. How fitting, since I'll be leaving my heart in Ireland.

A sign on the counter says Life Art won't work on anyone under the age of eighteen, either, but I'm armed with my note. The Head doesn't seem nearly as fussy as Ruby Tooth at Celestial Ring.

"I'd like one of those tiny clover tattoos," I tell him. "How much will it cost?"

"Twenty-five euros," he says, still without looking up. Then he asks, "You eighteen?"

Here we go. My hand is shaking as I hold out the folded purple note. "Just turned. And my mother gave me a letter of permission."

He waves it away and points to the couch. "Have a seat. Screech is in the back with a client."

My elation lasts exactly as long as it takes me to realize that the base of my spine is now totally out of the question. No one named Screech will be checking out my butt at close range. Or my belly for that matter. Besides, while twenty-five euros is a bargain compared to the rates at Celestial Ring, it will eat up a good part of the cash I have left.

Still, I can't chicken out now. I will focus instead on how the blood will drain from my mother's already pale face when she sees how I've mutilated my body. I will try to imagine what Abby would say if she were here now: *"It'll be so cool . . . Everyone will freak . . . It's so romantic . . . It's—"*

What was that noise? It sounds like a man's voice . . . moaning. The Head actually glances up at me briefly before cranking up the volume on the stereo. A few seconds later, I hear it again. It's more like a squeal this time and it's definitely coming from the back room. The squealing turns to yelling and a guy backs through the beaded curtain, shouting in a New York accent.

"Where did you study tattooing, man, the School of Medieval

Torture?" He already has several tattoos on his forearms and on his raised left hand is a work in progress. It looks like the bottom half of a mermaid. Turning to the Head, he says, "That dude is a menace."

Another man, who looks like the Head, only fatter and with more facial hair, pushes through the beads. This must be Screech.

"Relax, fella," Screech says. "I warned you it hurts worse around the bone. Come on back in and let me finish. You can't walk around with the arse-half of a mermaid." He snickers. "It's the boobs that count, right?"

When the squealer dashes out without paying, the Head shrugs at Screech and pulls out the design for my shamrock.

"Fer the love of humanity, would you turn down that racket?" A pretty woman who looks like one of the Corrs has just come in. Screech turns down the stereo as she steps behind the counter. "Got anything for me?"

"Nah, the kid's after ink, not a piercing."

A piercing! That's how I can avoid Screech, yet save face. Sure, I had my heart set on a tattoo, but a piercing still has shock value. And from the looks of the woman, it's bound to hurt a lot less. Checking the price list, I see it's also a lot cheaper. That settles it, I'll get a belly ring.

I'm about to tell the Head that I've changed my mind when the front door opens again and a girl even younger than I am arrives. "My belly ring's gone all funny," she announces, lifting up her T-shirt to reveal her scabby, festering navel. "It hurts like hell, you have no idea."

I'm out the door before the Head even turns around.

★　★　★

Terminal Burger is totally cool. At the front, there are computer terminals; at the back, there's a burger joint. And at a computer

near mine, there's a very cute guy playing Halo. While he's nowhere near as attractive as Sean, he is cute enough to make me reconsider my stance that only true geeks play computer games.

I forget about him soon enough, however, when I start my
e-mail to Abby. We haven't had much contact in the last couple of
weeks because I've been so distracted on set. Now I have a lot to
say. I tell her what's happened between Annika and Sean, admitting
I'm on the lam. I tell her that I love Sean—really, truly not-just-a-
crush love. I tell her that what I felt for Glen Myers wasn't even infatuation, it was so low-grade. I tell her that the heartbreak I've
experienced has aged me by several years. I tell her that I don't expect to love again. And I ask her how I can go back to school and
start grade eleven as if nothing has happened. My eyes well up as I
write.

I'm so focused on my story that I jump and nearly knock the
keyboard to the floor when a soft voice says, "What's that, your
autobiography?"

It's the cute guy and he's standing right beside me. Since I
can't get it together to minimize the screen, I drape myself casually
over the monitor. It doesn't look cool, but it's better than letting
him read about my sorry life. He seems to be about my age, with
wavy black shoulder-length hair, olive skin, and a totally buff bod.
His eyes are green—real green, not my muddy hazel—with thick,
long eyelashes. He has a stud in his eyebrow and two rings in
his ear.

"Uh, just a note to a friend." My voice is higher than usual.

"You've been typing for nearly an hour. That's some note."

He's been paying attention to what I'm doing! He couldn't care
that much about Halo. "Well, I haven't seen my friend in a long
time. A lot has happened."

"You're American?" he asks, stuffing his hands into the back
pockets of his baggy jeans.

I nod.

"Washington State?"

Okay, now I'm really impressed. "How did you know that?"

"My aunt lives in Seattle and you sound just like my cousins."

"Seattle's my hometown."

"I've been there twice. It's pretty cool."

"So's Dublin."

His name is Rory Quinn and he's smart and funny and nice. I find myself chatting with him quite easily. In fact, if it weren't for my burning face, it would be almost like talking to Abby. Mind you, I wouldn't care if my stomach growled in front of Abby, whereas when it lets out a roar so loud that Mrs. O could hear it back in Bray, my face becomes a ball of fire. Rory grins and offers to buy me a burger. I say I'll meet him at the back of the café as soon as I finish my e-mail; he warns me not to start another chapter.

Looking furtively over my shoulder to make sure he's safely at the food counter, I type:

Gotta go, Abby. The cute guy I mentioned is going to buy me a burger. I'm not interested in him. He's only 15 and I am attracted to more mature men, now. But I figure talking to him is good practice. One day, I may have a romantic scene in a movie and the more comfortable I am with guys, the less of a loser I'll be in front of the camera. And so, in the name of artistic research, I am off.

I'm surprised to discover that I can have a normal two-way conversation with a guy as cool as Rory. Even before our burgers arrive, we're discussing our favorite movies. I tell him that Abs and I have seen *Emma* fifteen times; he tells me he's seen *The Matrix* fifteen times. I tell him I hated *The Matrix*; he tells me no one could pay him enough to see *Emma*. But it doesn't seem to matter that we

don't like the same movies. Maybe it helps that I am already in love
with Sean and don't feel pressured to impress Rory. Besides, I know
that after today, I will never see this guy again. Whatever the reason, I find myself spilling my guts. I tell him about my parents' di-
vorce, about getting sent to Ireland, about being on the film set
with my mother. He really listens and asks lots of questions,
especially about my role in *Danny Boy*. It turns out that Rory is a total film buff.

The only thing I don't tell Rory about is Sean. Which is interesting. Why hold back on telling him about my broken heart when
I've shared everything else? But somehow I can't bear to have him
know that I lost my first true love to another woman—who also
happens to be my mother. It's too humiliating.

Two hours later, I feel like I know everything about him, yet I
want to know even more. He looks like he doesn't want to leave either, but he has to go to his summer job stocking shelves at Dunnes
grocery store in St. Stephen's Green shopping center. We exchange
e-mail addresses and phone numbers and he promises to let me
know the next time he visits his cousins.

As soon as he's out the door, I log back onto the computer and
update Abby:

> If I ever recovered from Sean and could love again, Rory would
> definitely be my type. It hurts me to say it, but Rory has more pol-
> ish than Sean. He didn't say one crude thing in two hours, which
> is more than Sean's ever managed. (That should get on Annika's
> nerves soon enough!)

> Rory hates our all-time favorite movie, Abs, but at least he's hon-
> est about it. I realize now that Sean only carried *Persuasion*
> around to impress Annika. It's so lame—although I fell for it too.
> And yes, I had Sean's Pogues CD in my Discman all last week,

but that was different because it was research for my character. Sinead may like the Pogues, but Leigh, not so much.

Anyway, I'd better go because I have to find somewhere to sleep tonight. Wish me luck!

My Rory high evaporates the minute I step out of Terminal Burger to find it's getting dark and pouring rain. I guess sleeping on a park bench is out of the question.

seventeen

A couple of rough-looking guys huddle against the wind and rain in the doorway of a boarded-up shop, sharing a smoke. Sensing they're watching me, I step hastily off the curb, triggering a loud clattering followed by a string of Irish obscenities: two skateboarders have swerved at the last second to avoid hitting me.

The creeps in the doorway are sniggering, but relief outweighs my embarrassment. The skateboards could as easily have been cars. I can't believe I've been here over a month and I still forget to look right first when I step into the road.

Half a block ahead, a slim, blond woman is struggling to keep an umbrella aloft, her head swiveling left and right. Although her hair is twisted into an unusually elegant knot, the Burberry umbrella is a dead giveaway: it's Annika.

"Mom!" I call. She doesn't turn, so I run toward her, my backpack slapping against my shoulder, and try again. *"Annika!"*

The woman turns with a puzzled look. It's not Annika; it's her younger, classier twin.

"Sorry, I thought you were someone else," I say.

I must look downhearted, because she smiles kindly. "Would you know where is La Caprice?" she asks. Make that Annika's younger, classier, *French* twin. "I am to meet friends there but I am lost."

Noting that the creepy guys have moved a few shop fronts closer to us, I offer to take the woman right to the door of La Caprice. The streets are so much busier in the Temple Bar area that the guys disappear into the crowd long before we reach the restaurant. Waving good-bye to the lady, I wander back up Grafton Street.

I can't believe I actually pursued someone I thought was Annika. You'd think I was desperate or something. Which I am not. I just got a little freaked out by those guys, is all. Besides, it's almost 9:00 and I still don't have a plan for the night. It didn't seem like a big deal this morning, but it's becoming bigger by the minute, especially in view of the rain. I refuse to sleep in an alley under a cardboard box. Sure, I need all kinds of experiences to help me mature as an actress, but I don't imagine I'll be cast as a bag lady anytime soon. I'll leave those roles for Annika.

I have to admit, I expected her to come after me by now. I figured she'd be shamed into it by Mrs. O'Reilly, or Colleen, or maybe even Dad. She could have found me if she'd made the slightest effort; the city isn't that big and there aren't that many places a teen would go. By all rights, I should be sulking on my cot in Bray, already—disgraced, but warm and dry.

What kind of a mother leaves her kid to spend a night alone in a strange city, anyway? The rotten kind—the same kind who'd abandon her kid for a life in Tinseltown. The only mystery here is why I expected anything more. Before Ireland, I never expected anything from Annika, other than the occasional phone call and some extravagant, off-the-mark gifts. But hearing her snore for nearly six weeks duped me into thinking she's actually human. Recently, she's seemed more than human, almost decent. I should never have let her get around me. No expectations, no disappointments.

Running away hasn't punished her at all. Rather, it's played right into her hands. Tonight she'll take full advantage of her freedom to have a romantic dinner with Sean. In fact, they're probably at La

Caprice right now. I should have popped in to say hello. No doubt they're telling each other that I'll be on the last train home to Bray with my tail between my legs.

Well, they don't know Leigh Reid very well. I am not giving up. Did Scarlett O'Hara give up in *Gone with the Wind*? No, she did not. When her life was falling apart around her, she became more determined than ever to succeed. *"As God is my witness, they're not going to lick me!"* she said. *"I'm going to live through this and when it's all over, I'll never be hungry again!"*

Okay, so I'm not exactly hungry, having eaten a burger an hour ago, but if I'm spending the night alone in the big city, I can't count on Mrs. O'Reilly to fry up my breakfast. I'd better be resourceful, like Scarlett. Under this matted hair is a superior brain; I've just been feeling too sorry for myself to use it. I will come up with a solution that will not include crawling back to Bray. If and when I see my mother again, I will be rested, clean, and confident. Even if I don't have a tattoo.

My first stop must be the Bank of Ireland. My superior brain is telling me that solutions cost money. Fortunately, I still have a couple of thousand dollars in *Danny Boy* earnings in my account and I am prepared to spend what I have to so that I can live in high style until my plane leaves for the States. There will be plenty of time to save for college later. Tonight, I will book myself into Bono's Clarence Hotel, have a hot bath, and wrap myself in a big, fluffy robe to watch movies on TV. I'll call room service and order a sundae. And hot chocolate. Then tomorrow I'll get a blow-out at the hotel salon and tell Roger to send a driver to collect me for Sinead's final scene.

This is such a great scenario that I find myself humming U2's "One" as I walk up Parliament Street. I'm thinking of my one true love, now lost to me forever.

Sean should get a stud in his eyebrow like Rory's. He could

afford to be a little cooler. Maybe he'd even get some play in the U.S. movie magazines.

★ ★ ★

YOU HAVE REACHED YOUR DAILY MAXIMUM FOR THIS ACCOUNT.

There must be some mistake. Maybe I punched in the wrong PIN number. Rubbing my hands together to thaw them, I try again. The card pops out abruptly, as if the machine is sticking its tongue out at me.

YOU HAVE REACHED YOUR DAILY MAXIMUM FOR THIS ACCOUNT.

With a sinking feeling, I remember that my Former Mother imposed a daily withdrawal limit of $100 euros. I didn't complain at the time: 100 euros seemed like a lot and there was nothing much to buy in Bray anyway.

Okay, so I'm down, but I am not out. I will call the Clarence and see what the forty-five euros I still have left can buy me.

I sense the sundae and blow-out fading from my scenario. Hopefully, I can still afford the hot chocolate.

★ ★ ★

The phone booth smells of urine. I tell myself it's dog urine, because the alternative is too disgusting. Next time I run away, I'll recharge my cell phone first.

"Clarence Hotel. How may I help you?"

"I'd like to book a room, please."

"Wonderful. For one?"

"That's right. For tonight."

"For tonight! We're fully booked, ma'am. Peak season, you know."

Ma'am! Is he making fun of me? "Would you mind double-checking?"

"Well, I do have one suite left. Would that do?"

"I guess. How much is it?"

"Six hundred and fifty euros."

My response comes out as a strangled squawk. "Oh my god."

"There is a discount for the corporate traveler."

★ ★ ★

"Emerald Isle Youth Hostel."

"I'd like to book a room, please."

"We don't have private rooms, love, just dorms. Six or ten to a dorm."

And I thought sharing a room with Annika was bad. "What are your rates?"

"Twenty-eight euros for the six-bed dorm, and twenty-two for the ten. No sheets, but breakfast included."

Who needs sheets? I have my pride to keep me warm. "I'll take the six-bed option—for tonight, please."

"Sorry, fully booked, love. It's—"

"—peak season, I know."

★ ★ ★

"Shamrock Hostel, Aemon speaking."

"Hi, Aemon, do you have any beds for tonight?"

"Just one, I'm afraid. In the mixed dorm."

"Mixed?"

"Men and women. Ten beds to a room."

Ugh. An alley might not be so bad. At least I could have my own cardboard box.

"That sounds terrific, Aemon. How much will it cost?"

"Nineteen euros."

"I'll be there in half an hour."

"Just for your information, we always ask for identification at the front desk."

"Uh, why?"

"For starters, anyone under eighteen must be accompanied by an adult. Hostel policy."

Make that *hostile* policy. "So anyone under eighteen is supposed to sleep in an alley?"

Aemon's voice is gentle when he says, "The thinking behind the policy is that young people should be staying with adults. You'll find it's the same in all the hostels."

"Great news."

"How about staying with a friend?"

"I don't have any friends, Aemon."

★ ★ ★

Actually, I have two friends in Dublin. Since I am not about to admit to Rory that I am a street person, I decide to call Siobhan. Digging the slip of paper she gave me out of my pocket, I slide another coin into the payphone.

"Hi, Siobhan, it's Leigh—the girl you met this morning outside Trinity College." There's a lot of noise on her end of the phone and I don't hear a reply. Raising my voice, I add, "You know, the one reading *Angela's Ashes*?"

"Right," she says, although it doesn't sound like she remembers. "Howya?"

"Good. I went to see the *Book of Kells* like you said."

"I can't hear you, there's such a racket here. Can you shout?"

So much for the subtle approach. Well, the clock is ticking, so I might as well go for it.

"I was supposed to sleep in my cousin's dorm tonight but she forgot I was coming and isn't there." *(I'm a genius!)* "I don't really know anyone yet so I was wondering if I could crash on your floor? Just for tonight, I promise."

"You're welcome anytime," she says. Relief floods through me in a wave. "There's just one thing . . ." Uh-oh, don't tell me she has an adults-only policy, too. "We're having a bit of a hooley, here. Been at it since four."

A hooley? Whatever it is, it sounds like fun. There are lots of voices in the background.

I scribble the directions on the same slip of paper and set off. Hanging out with college kids is an experience I'll definitely be able to use.

★　★　★

I would never have thought that so many people could cram into a one-room apartment. The only way I can fit through the door is by taking off my backpack first. I drop it with the pile coats and bags in the hallway outside the door and inch into the room.

Siobhan, when I find her, is sitting in the kitchen sink, a beer in one hand, a cigarette in the other.

"Hey, great to see you!" she says. "I'd give you a hug, but I think I'm stuck here for the rest of the night. At least when I have to pee, I'm all set."

"Thanks for letting me come. I really appreciate it."

"I could have sworn you were Irish this morning. No wonder I didn't recognize you on the phone."

Of course. She met *Sinead.* I must be getting tired, because I'm starting to lose track of my lies. "Sorry, I'm practicing my American accent for a part in a movie."

She laughs. "Don't worry, I've had so much to drink I'd believe anything you say."

Which is a good thing, or she'd be wondering why I wouldn't just go home to my parents tonight. "No really, I'm an actress," I insist, switching into Sinead's accent.

"Aren't we all?" she says, laughing even harder. "Have a beer and relax, will you? Michael, get this one a drink."

A nerdy-looking guy pushes out of a tight spot in the corner and brings me a plastic cup of warm beer from a huge silver keg.

Taking a big swig, I find it's even more disgusting than the strong tea I drank on set that day. I wipe my mouth with the back of my hand and manage to smile.

"Thanks, er, Michael," I say, suddenly aware of how bad I must look. I haven't showered in two days and I'm so damp I'm moldering like dead leaves in November. I probably smell like a mushroom.

Michael doesn't seem to notice it, but judging by his extraloud voice, he doesn't find the beer as nasty as I do, either. "So, where are you from, exactly?" he asks. "I don't recognize that accent."

Since Siobhan is busy talking to someone else, I say, "Belfast—but I've spent the past few years in America. I came back this summer to shoot a movie."

"A movie, how *interesting.*" He is standing a little too close to me, but then, it's hard to get much personal space in here.

"It's not that interesting," I say, edging away. "It's a very small role."

"What part do you play?" He puts his hand on my arm and stares into my eyes as if I'm totally fascinating. I guess that's what the term *beer goggles* means.

I tell him about *Danny Boy,* rambling on about the tiniest details in the hopes that he'll get bored and find someone else to back into the wall. On the contrary, he seems riveted by the story. I see now that there were some advantages to being unable to have a conversation with guys. Mastering "small talk" opens up a whole new set of problems.

Michael is probably a year or two younger than Sean, but I feel uncomfortable with him. That's probably because I was just hanging out with Rory, who is exactly my age. Or maybe it's because Sean is immature. At any rate, Michael seems old. Why would he waste his time talking to me when there are so many girls his own age in the room who do not smell like fungus? I haven't a clue how to escape him, either. If I ever see Colleen again, I'll remember to ask her about making a polite getaway.

The beer is so thick and foamy that I almost choke on it and when I lower my glass, a loud burp slips out against my will. Horrified, I cover my mouth and apologize, but amazingly, Michael doesn't seem to notice. He's staring at the long bathroom lineup that snakes along the wall. That's it! The perfect excuse. My escape route, however, is blocked by a very large, very drunk man, who mumbles incoherently as he lumbers in my direction.

"Watch out, Leigh," Siobhan calls over. "Those Texan exchange students don't know how to hold their liquor." Tex veers to the left just in time and crashes into the wall. Sliding down the wall into a sitting position, he closes his eyes.

"Is he okay?" I ask Siobhan anxiously.

She nods. "It looks like you'll have company on the floor tonight. But don't worry, he's harmless."

Staying here no longer seems like such a great idea. It's after ten o'clock, yet more people are arriving all the time. There's a cigarette in almost every hand and the smoke is hanging in a dense cloud. A girl offers me a puff of her cigarette while I stand in the bathroom line, but I shake my head. Maybe I'd be more adventurous if I'd had some sleep last night, but right now all I really want to do is go to bed. Besides, my episode with the cigar didn't exactly leave me wanting more.

Michael brings me another beer just before my turn in the bathroom. I pour it down the drain. What's with these people? Even when Fin does my makeup and Mary and Maude dress me, I know I don't look like a college student. And in my muddy jeans and T-shirt tonight, I look more like twelve. What do they think I am, a prodigy? Two years from now, when I'm in college myself, I will have to remind myself of how gullible students are, especially when there's beer involved. For tonight, I'm cutting myself off.

Stepping out of the bathroom, I make a beeline to the door. I grab my backpack and run down the stairs. It's only when I am on the sidewalk again that I realize my bag is unusually light. I open it to find that my wallet is gone, as well as all three of my novels. Amazingly, my airplane ticket and passport are still in the side pouch.

Panic swells in my throat, but I try all my pockets, hoping against hope that I stashed some cash in there at some point today. And sure enough, when I get to the zippered pocket of my hoodie, I find my bank card and a twenty euro bill. I can still cover the fare back to Bray.

It's starting to look like I'll be on the last train after all. Although the bank machine will likely consider it a new day at 12:01 and cough up another $100 euros, how will it really help me? Yes, I could still call Rory, but he lives with his parents and they'd insist on calling my mother. I'd rather go home on my own steam than get ratted out. That way, I can pretend I had a choice.

My eyes may be running, but I am not crying. That "hooley" was a smoke pit. And what kind of loser steals novels? A loser getting a higher education, that's who.

eighteen

I decide to spend my last hour of freedom in Meeting House Square, where Mom and I watched the Celtic drummers perform yesterday. It's hard to believe that so much has changed in less than two days. When we sat side by side on this bench yesterday, I was actually comfortable with Annika for the first time ever. It seemed that we might have some hope of getting along someday. Now that she's betrayed me, I guess we'll go back to two tense phone calls a year—at least until I'm old enough to get an unlisted phone number.

Sitting here yesterday was more comfortable for other reasons, too. Specifically, the sun was shining. Now it's raining so hard I can barely see two feet in front of me. Not that there's anything to see in the dark, empty square—except for my own defeat. Sure, there's still a slight chance that my superior brain will come up with a last-ditch plan, but I sense that my tail is between my legs. In fact, I'm sitting on it now, as I mentally prepare a script for the ugly scene that waits in Bray.

Suddenly, the rain stops above me and I look up to find an enormous Burberry umbrella over my head. This time, it's in the hand of the real Annika. Her curls are jutting all over in damp, crazy corkscrews and her Glazed Poppy lipstick has worn off, leaving a faint, waxy line around her mouth. In short, she looks like crap, which makes me happier than I've felt all day.

"Vivien," she says, "I don't even know where to start."

"How about starting with an apology?" As relieved as I am that she's saved me the humiliation of crawling back to Bray, I'm not about to call it even.

"You must be joking!" Her stunned expression would make me laugh if I weren't so cold and miserable. "I've been sitting here all day in the pouring rain and this is what you have to say?"

"All day?" What she probably means is "for the past hour, after cocktails with Sean."

"Yes, *all day*. Lucky dropped me off here at ten o'clock this morning and I've been waiting ever since."

"You've been here for nearly thirteen hours?" Dad must have threatened her with legal action.

"I didn't think you'd hold out until the last train. I forgot how stubborn you are."

"Who says I'm taking the last train? I'm still weighing my options."

"Really. You couldn't weigh them somewhere warm and dry?"

"I'm resting. I've had a very busy day, what with shopping, making new friends, visiting tattoo shops . . . I even went to a party with college kids."

"Don't forget your visit to the Burger Terminal."

"*Terminal Burger.* And how did you know?"

"Mrs. MacKenzie called your father after Abby got your e-mail."

"Abby's a traitor!"

"She did the right thing. At least we knew you were still alive at dinnertime."

"Well, why have you been waiting here?"

"I figured you'd show up eventually. I'm not completely lacking in mother's intuition, you know."

"Could have fooled me."

Her cell phone rings. She digs it out of her handbag to glance at the number and then drops it back in without answering. Must be Sean, wondering if they can hook up after she gets this nasty bit of business settled. "Colleen told me what happened. You misunderstood what you saw last night."

"I saw you sneaking into a hotel with Sean's arm around you. What's to misunderstand about that?"

"Vivien, do I really seem like the type of woman who'd sneak off to a hotel room with a twenty-one year old?" She stares at the side of my head because I refuse to look at her.

"How would I know what type of woman you are? I barely know you."

She draws the collar of her trench coat up around her chin. "Well, I've never had to sneak around, I can assure you of that. Annika Anderson always walks in with her head held high."

Her cell phone rings again. "Why don't you just pick it up? I know it's Sean."

She takes the phone out of her purse and hits a button. "Officer, I've found her! Yes, she's fine. It was just a rebellious teen moment. I can't thank you enough for your help." There's a pause and then, "Really? Why thank you, you're too kind." Smiling, she pushes a strand a limp hair behind her ear and bats her eyelashes. "Why yes, of course. It would be my pleasure! Drop by the set tomorrow then."

Unbelievable. Even under these conditions she can manage to flirt. "You called the police?"

"Of course. Anything could have happened to you."

"And now you're going to two-time Sean and date the cop?"

She jerks the umbrella away from my head and covers only herself. "Officer Malone would like my autograph, actually. And I am not dating Sean. Not, I might add, that it is any of your business."

I can't believe what I'm hearing. "It's not my business that you went to a hotel with my boyfriend?"

"If you really think Sean is your boyfriend, you *do* need that mother-daughter talk I mentioned when you first got here."

Ouch! She is so asking for it. "First I'll need a mother to give it to me."

The big umbrella wobbles as she slumps forward on the bench. Hah! A direct hit! But she keeps her voice level as she continues. "You and Sean aren't having a relationship, Vivien."

"Well, you knew how I felt about him. Any normal mother would have backed off."

"Knowing how you felt would have stopped me from seeing him—if I'd wanted to see him in the first place."

"Oh please, you were always flirting with him."

"Flirting with men is one of the great joys of a woman's life. Besides, with Roger behaving so badly, I couldn't help but enjoy Sean's attention. That doesn't mean I was dating him."

"Then what were you doing last night?"

"I had dinner with Sean—"

"How could you!" I jump to my feet, nearly poke my eye out on her Burberry, and sink back down.

Her mouth twitches, but she finishes her sentence. "—and Sean's cousin, Anthony." A likely story. She's had all day to make up a good script and this is the best she can do? I hate her. "Anthony and his wife run one of the hottest acting schools in Los Angeles. They've developed something called the 'Reality Method.' Since they're here on a visit, I asked Sean to set up a meeting so we could talk about it."

"More acting lessons aren't going to help, Annie."

Amazingly, she doesn't rise to the bait. Maybe she's on some sort of medication.

"I may be too old for new methods," she agrees, "but you aren't."

"So what? It's not like I'm ever in L.A." I've never been invited.

"The school has a summer course for teens that's booked long in advance. I wanted to talk them into letting you in next year."

I have no reason to believe her, yet somehow I sense that she's telling the truth. "Well, why all the secrecy?"

"I didn't want to get your hopes up if I couldn't persuade them."

I feel myself weakening. I can't help it. I'd love to spend a summer in California, as long as it didn't require selling my soul to the devil. "Did it work?"

She smiles, thinking she's won the battle. I must resist. Leigh Reid cannot be bought with acting classes. There are plenty of acting schools in Seattle and I don't need her help.

"They'll accept you only if I agree to their ridiculous terms."

I'm curious, although I try to sound bored. "What terms?"

"In December, their junior class puts on a show for the American Actor's Guild Christmas party. A professional actor mentors the students and takes a lead role in the show. This year they're doing *The Wizard of Oz* and they want me to participate."

"What, as the Wicked Witch of the West?"

I'm just being mean, but she nods. "I'm afraid so."

"So you refused."

"On the contrary. I get to wear a wig, a false nose, blackened teeth, and warts. It's the opportunity of a lifetime."

I try to muffle a laugh in my sleeve, but she grins, too. My mother has rarely looked less than stunning in any role. If she is willing to appear in front of her peers in that costume, maybe she actually does want me to come to L.A. next summer. Still, I am skeptical. "I thought you didn't want me to act."

"Watching you do so well has been hard for me, I can't deny it. Acting seems to come easily to you, whereas I've trained and struggled for twenty-five years only to land a string of average roles. In fact, *Danny Boy* is the first movie of substance that I've done. But that's my problem, not yours, and if acting is what you want to do, I'm going to support you."

I can hardly believe my ears. Is she really putting me first? Being a real mom? There has to be an angle. "I might still become a vet."

"You might become an astronaut, who knows? This course just allows you to explore one of your options. Besides, you'll get to see L.A."

"Where would I stay?" I'm careful not to commit to anything until I know all the details.

"I'm not putting you up at a hotel, if that's what you're thinking."

"But I've never been to your place."

"That was your father's decision, not mine. He felt it would disrupt your life too much."

"He never told me that."

She sighs. "It's not all his fault. Maybe I didn't push hard enough. I honestly thought you were better off with him and your grandmother in Seattle."

"He'll never let me come, especially not after today."

"Do you think I'd agree to warts—*warts, Vivien*—if I didn't already have his okay?"

I laugh again, but suddenly my eyes fill up. I'm so tired that I'm getting delirious. Fortunately, the rain running down my face won't give me away. "Thanks, Mom."

"You're welcome, Vivien."

"Leigh," I say, but with a lot less tone than usual. "Look, are you going to keep hogging that umbrella?"

★   ★   ★

We pick up sandwiches at the train station. I've never seen my mother eat a whole sandwich before, but she does it now, and in record time. To prove she hasn't had an entire personality makeover, however, she insists we stand outside to wait for the train in case anyone from the production comes by.

"I have never looked worse," she says.

"But you will, witchie-poo."

"Watch it, I can still change my mind." She smiles as she accepts a large piece of my chocolate bar.

While Mom calls Mrs. O'Reilly to say we're on our way, I pull my booklet about the *Book of Kells* out of my backpack. Thankfully, the thief at the party thumbed his nose at Irish history and left my souvenir.

"I almost got one of these tattooed on my back today," I tell Annika, pointing to a particularly complicated design, "but they wouldn't do it without parental consent."

"You might want to go with something more subtle," she says. "This would cover half your back."

Thank god I didn't risk gangrene at Life Art for such a disappointing reaction. "Aren't you shocked that I'd mutilate my body?" I'm already starting to hope that she might let me get the tiny shamrock.

"I'm more worried about the party you mentioned. I smell liquor and I don't recall your reaching legal age overnight."

"I had one sip of warm beer," I explain as we board the train. "It was disgusting."

The phone rings again as we get off the train in Bray. There's a raised male voice on the other end but it isn't loud enough for me to identify it. Roger maybe? I listen to my mother's side of the conversation. "She's fine. Didn't Mrs. O'Reilly call you? Yes, well I didn't think now was the best— Why don't you call in the— I understand, but it's been a difficult—" The volume of the voice on the other end increases sharply and my mother pulls the phone away from her ear. Now there's no mistaking the voice. She passes me the phone.

"Hi, Dad!" I chirp. Maybe when he hears how happy I am, he'll lighten up.

"I have never been more disappointed," he says.

"Give her a break, Dad, it was just a misunderstanding."

"Her! This is not about your mother, it's about you. How could you?"

"Me! I just spent the day in town on my own, no big deal—"

"Vivien." Uh-oh, Dad never calls me Vivien. "How could you be so irresponsible? Disappearing like that—and in a strange country no less! Do you know what you've put us through? Do you realize how frantic your mother has been? She has half the population of Ireland on high alert, from the police to the movie's director."

"Oh my god—that's totally embarrassing!"

"Embarrassing? You don't seem to grasp how serious this is. How can I trust you if you run off when you get upset? Your mother wants you to study at some fancy acting school next summer, but I can't risk your running away in a city like L.A."

"But I wouldn't," I protest, climbing after Mom into the backseat of Lucky's car.

He continues as if I didn't interrupt. "And don't tell me that this was her fault. She already tried it and it doesn't wash with me. You're even more of a drama queen than she is. I don't know what happened to my share of your genes." I look over at my mother, surprised to hear she took the blame for my running off. "You're always telling me to treat you like an adult, but then you pull a stunt like this. Being an adult means working out your problems when the going gets tough."

"The way you and Mom did?" Oops. It's out before I have a chance to stop it. My father is silent on the other end of the phone and beside me, Annika stiffens. I try throwing myself on the grenade before it explodes. "Look, Dad, I'm sorry. I didn't mean it. I'm just really, really tired. It's been a long day." I cross my fingers, hoping he'll let it drop.

"Fine, but don't think this is the end of the discussion, young lady. We'll be talking about this for a very long time."

After saying good-bye, I hand the phone back to my mother and say, "I think he took that well."

She waits a beat and then cracks up.

★　★　★

Mrs. O'Reilly is chain smoking on the porch with Skip at her side when Lucky pulls up. She's wearing the new bathrobe she bought in Cork, to be worn only for special occasions. I'm honored.

"Come 'ere, ye daft child," she says, wrapping her arms around me so tight I nearly black out. How weird, when she's never seemed exactly fond of me. "Everyone's been on the hoof searching for you."

"Who's everyone?" I look at my mother. "You said you used 'mother's intuition' to find me."

"Well, I'm out of practice. I needed a few spies on the ground as backup. Mary and Maude waited at the beach, Fin was at La Caprice, Colleen spent the day at the Clarence Hotel, Sean covered Grafton Street, Roger waited at the studio in case you showed and Mrs. O'Reilly held the fort here."

Mrs. O adds proudly, "Even Mr. O'Reilly pulled himself away from the Thirsty Leprechaun to patrol the train station."

I am ashamed of putting so many people to so much trouble. I wish I didn't have to face them again tomorrow. For the moment, however, I am so tired that I can block it out.

★   ★   ★

Or not. Once I'm under the covers, I'm too wired to sleep.

"I can't go to set tomorrow," I tell my mother. "How will I face everyone?"

"It won't be so bad." Her voice is foggy with sleep. "They're happy you're safe. Remember, they were impulsive teenagers once, too."

Then another thought hits me. Tomorrow we shoot the final scene of the movie and it's my most demanding scene yet. "How am I going to get through my lines? I haven't reviewed them in days. My mind has gone completely blank!"

"You'll be fine," she says. "You've read them a hundred times and they'll be there when you need them. Trust me."

"But—"

"Get some sleep, Vivien."

"What if they don't come back?"

"They will, I promise."

"What if I freeze?"

"Relax, you can do it."

I find myself sinking into sleep and struggle to resist. "Mom?"

"What now?"

"At the party, someone stole my books and two of them were on loan from Sean."

Her voice is suddenly alert in the darkness. "What did I tell you? *Never* leave your bag unattended in public. You're lucky it was only your books."

I decide not to mention the wallet just yet. After all, she's had a long day, too.

nineteen

Annika is already up and dressed when I roll over onto my back. Her suitcases are open on her bed and she's carefully layering her clothes between sheets of tissue paper. She'd better not nag me to start packing, because we still have two whole days left. It's funny: I spent weeks looking forward to going home and now that the time has almost arrived, I'm in no hurry. Sure, I'll be glad to see Grandma and Millie—and even Dad—but going back to school will be such a drag. At least I can look forward to spending next summer in Hollywood. I haven't actually agreed to go, but unless Mom reverts into Annika the Irritating between now and then, I probably will. Otherwise, Dad will make me get a summer job.

Noticing I'm awake, Annika says, "I'm going to need an extra suitcase. What do you say we go into Dublin tomorrow to pick up a few things?"

"Can I get something to wear for the wrap party?" I ask.

"Didn't you buy enough the other day?"

"I didn't get anything dressy. Please?"

"We'll see." She raises her eyebrows in the you-haven't-really-earned-it look. It's amazing how quickly she's picked up the bad habits of a real parent. By next summer, I won't be able to get away with much. Knowing her, she's probably already signed up for classes on "Managing Your Teenager."

"I tried on some things at Envy yesterday," I tell her. "But it's the kind of stuff Grandma never lets me wear, so maybe it's not a good idea."

Mom likes nothing better than sticking it to Grandma. "I suppose we could take a look. You'll want to look your best at the party."

For today, at least, I can still get around her. Time to test deeper waters: "Have you thought anymore about the tattoo?"

"What tattoo?" She looks deliberately mystified.

"I mentioned it last night. I want to get a tiny shamrock with a heart inside."

"You're not getting a tattoo. I've pushed my luck far enough with your father."

That's not an absolute no. I sense there's room for maneuvering here. "You should see it, Mom, it's so cute."

"I don't need to see it; you're not getting a tattoo. No debate, Vivien."

"But it would help me remember my summer in Ireland."

"You're always mentioning your amazing memory, so you're not likely to have much trouble. I'd be happy to fill in any blanks for you."

I can see from the way she's snapping the tissue paper that she's enjoying herself. I think her parenting skills are coming along a little too well. Maybe I was wrong to assume I got my brains from Dad. "I had this great idea, Mom. What if we got *matching* tattoos?"

"You can't be serious. Let me be perfectly clear: I would never—*never*—mutilate my body with a tattoo." She drops the skirt she's folding to glower at me.

Score one point for Leigh. I cross my arms behind my head on the pillow. "Why not? It's tiny and you could cover it with makeup when you're filming. I checked with Fin."

"I don't need to be worrying about whether my tattoo is showing—especially in love scenes. It's hard enough getting naked in front of the camera."

I wince at the mental image and she grins: score one point for Annika.

"Fine. I just thought it would be nice if we had a souvenir of our first summer together."

"We'll get matching T-shirts instead."

"You're right, it was a stupid idea," I say, getting out of bed. "Hardly anyone over forty can pull off a tattoo anyway."

Tossing a sweater on the bed, she stalks out of the room. Another point for Leigh! Playing the age card is far too easy, but with only two days left there's no time for the subtle approach.

★   ★   ★

Mrs. O has outdone herself. In addition to the usual breakfast fry-up, there's oatmeal and a fresh loaf of soda bread.

"Eat it," she says when I cast a skeptical glance at the thick, lumpy porridge. "You'll need your strength today for your apologies."

Apologies? Who said anything about apologies? My plan is to pretend nothing happened yesterday and carry on like it's business as usual. If anyone mentions it, I will *act* oblivious. Pretty soon I'll be gone and I'll never see these people again.

But Mrs. O'Reilly is a lot better than my mother at reading my blank stare. "If yer big enough to run away to Dublin, young wan, yer big enough to do the right thing upon yer return."

"I'm not apologizing. Like Mom said, I'm a rebellious teenager and they were all teenagers once too."

Mrs. O puts butter and salt on my porridge, knowing full well that I prefer it sweet. It's her way of making a statement. As if having Dad rant on about "acting like an adult" isn't bad enough. Ireland is a free country and I have the right not to be lectured.

Sliding the bowl in front of me, she says, "Now, save room for 'humble pie.' You'll be eating a lot of it later."

Shrugging an unspoken "whatever" at her, I stick my spoon into the stiff porridge.

★ ★ ★

There must be advantages to acting like an adult, but at the moment, I can't see what they are. My first hour at the studio is the hardest I've spent here, with or without the cameras rolling. I've been making my rounds to apologize to everyone. People have mostly been nice about it. Colleen hugged me, Roger said he was glad I'm safe, and Finian actually *thanked* me: he had a great time at La Caprice on Mom's tab, especially after running into Lord Tracy. Mary and Maude, however, spent the day patrolling the beach in the rain and are less understanding. As a gesture, I offer to help them pack up the enormous wardrobe trailer after we wrap. It's not that big a sacrifice, since Sinead's dress clothes might be up for grabs.

Having saved the worst for last, I finally knock on the door of Sean's trailer. Mom didn't say, but I suspect she's told him why I ran away, which means that this will be totally humiliating. Still, I'd rather face him here than on set, in front of cast and crew.

"It's open, Maude," he calls. The door swings back to reveal piles of clothes everywhere, half-eaten meals on the table, and bottles rolling on the floor. When I locate Sean in the debris, he's wearing only boxer shorts covered in tiny sheep. "Jaysus!" He grabs a rumpled pair of jeans from a pile and pulls them on. "I thought you were Maude with my wardrobe trousers."

A week ago, the sight of Sean in his boxers would have rated an immediate text message to Abby. Today, I'm just grateful that he's embarrassed, too. It makes me feel like less of a fool. "This place is a sty, Sean."

"I know. The drivers refuse to clean more than once a week."

"Doing it yourself would be out of the question?"

His white teeth gleam in the dark trailer. "If my career goes as planned, I will never clean again."

I shake my head. "I thought you were in this business to create art."

"Sure, but I won't say no to perks like a housekeeper."

His smile still makes my heart beat a little faster, but I can't help noticing that his bare arms and chest are on the scrawny side. Some weight training wouldn't kill him. He'll never get big action roles if he looks like the heaviest thing he lifts is a pint.

Catching me staring, Sean reaches for a shirt. My face starts a slow burn, but before I can give in to the urge to bolt, I force myself to spit out my apology. "Sean, I'm really sorry for putting you out yesterday. I had no idea everyone would worry if I took off. I just wanted a day on my own."

"*I* wasn't worried," he says, still grinning. "I figured Roger could use a computer-generated Sinead today if you didn't come back. It would be less trouble than acting opposite the real one."

I laugh, grateful he's making this easier for me. "That's probably the best way to go: I'm nervous I might blow it today."

"Ah, you'll be fine. You just needed to get that out of your system so you could focus."

By "that," I sense he means "him." And judging by the fact that he hasn't buttoned his shirt, I think he's flattered. Well, he needn't think I'm heartbroken, or anything. In fact, I've already moved on and I'd better let him know it. "I had an *amazing* day in Dublin. I saw the *Book of Kells* and shopped and hung out at a cybercafe. I even met a nice guy and had dinner with him."

"But what would Devin Bainbridge say?"

"I'm over Devin."

"Already? Well done. And who's the new guy? Another brainiac?"

"He is pretty smart. And cute, too."

"Sounds like a wanker."

"Shut up! He's great. And he's exactly my age."

"Ah, so you're putting the 'old perv' thing behind you."

So he *does* know. There's no point in dodging it now. "You're not *old*, Sean—just a perv."

"Hey! Don't be letting *that* get around." Laughing, he tries to take a swing at me as I back toward the door.

"You know what would help your image?"

"I don't take advice from kids."

"Piercings—and lots of them."

"Pierce this face? I don't think so."

Geez, he's as conceited as my mother. What is it with actors? "You'd look a lot cooler, I'm just saying."

"What you're really saying is that you're too cool for me."

"Right now I am, but it might wear off by the time I'm *your age*."

"Well, when you're my age give me a call and I'll take you for a proper drink."

"*You* call *me* and I'll think about it."

Annika is off base about so many things, but she has a point about the flirting.

Danny Boy: Scene 152

Friends and relatives have gathered in the O'Leary house to bid Danny good-bye. He is leaving with Fiona for New York City the next day. Mr. and Mrs. O'Leary have reluctantly invited Fiona to join the festivities.

As the scene opens, Sinead enters from the kitchen carrying a tray. The camera tracks with her across the crowded living room to Fiona.

The props guy hands me a huge, heavy silver tray of blueberry tarts. As Roger calls action, I push open the fake kitchen door with the tray and stagger clumsily into the living room set. The camera pulls back with me as I weave through the crowd, offering tarts to people until I reach Annika.

                    SINEAD
          Try a blueberry tart, Fiona. My grand-
          mother's recipe.

                    FIONA
          Oh yes, I remember them. They're my fa-
          vorite.

Annika selects a tart and takes a microscopic bite. The muscles in my arms are quivering under the weight of the tray and I'm afraid I may drop it. Looking around for a table, I see the props guy standing behind the camera, smirking. This must be his revenge for my disastrous first day on set.

Touching my arm to bring me back to earth, Annika ad-libs a line to cover for the fact that I've dropped mine.

                    FIONA
          Delicious! Perhaps I'll have another tart.

                    SINEAD
          Have another tart. Perhaps they're deli-
          cious.

My stomach sinks. I'm screwing up my last scene and in seconds Roger will—

"*Cut!*" Roger bellows, removing his headphones. To my surprise, he doesn't yell at me. Instead, he turns to the props guy: "How about giving the kid a tray smaller than a football field, you idiot?"

Still smirking, the guy replaces my tray with a small plastic one that just happens to be fully loaded with tarts already.

"I wanted to be perfect on my last day," I whisper to Annika, "but I'm already blowing it."

"Shake it off, Vivien. You've got to focus."

Her complete lack of sympathy makes it possible for me to walk away without mentioning the chunk of blueberry wedged between her front teeth. As I return to my starting position, however, Finian sails by me carrying dental floss.

"And . . . Action!"

I carry the new tray over to Annika. After she says her line and selects a tart, I set the tray on the side table the props guy has now set up.

> SINEAD
> Blueberry tarts are Danny's favorite too.
> You'd know that if you'd been around all
> his life.

> FIONA
> You're right, I've missed a lot. That's why
> I'm so happy he's coming to New York. Now I
> can learn everything about him.

The camera follows Fiona as she crosses the room to speak to Kathleen.

I wait for my cue and then take my place beside Sean on the sofa.

> DANNY
> What do you think of Fiona?

> SINEAD
> She's ruining everything, that's what I
> think! You were fine without her. I don't
> see why you'd follow her halfway around

the world when she's never bothered with
you before now. If Fiona really cared,
she'd have come sooner.

The lines were all in my head, just like Annika promised. But
the funny thing is that they don't even seem like lines—they seem
like my own thoughts. And no matter how hard I try, I can't stop
my voice from shaking.

Danny puts down his beer and sighs.

> DANNY
> I understand how you feel, Sinead, but I'm
> trying to see it from her perspective. She
> was young when she had me and she didn't
> feel up to raising a kid. She says I was
> better off with our da and maybe she's
> right. I want to believe that she's sorry
> for leaving me behind so I'm trying to let
> go of the past and think about the future.

My eyes fill and overflow as I listen to Sean. It feels so real that
I can't stop myself.

> SINEAD
> I'll miss you, Danny. It won't be the same
> without you.

Sean's eyes mist, too.

> DANNY
> I'll miss you too, kid. But nothing stays
> the same, you know. Things change. People

```
change. You'll change. Come visit me in New
York and you may even stay.

                    SINEAD
I'll visit you, but I'll never stay. I'm
Irish through and through.
```

"Cut," Roger says.

Finian rushes in with tissues for Sean and me. For a moment, there's silence in the studio and I wonder if Roger is mad that I broke down. Then, on the other side of the set, someone starts clapping. I turn to see that it's Annika. Everyone else joins in.

"You nailed it, guys," Roger calls to us over the hubbub. Turning to the rest of the cast and crew, he announces, "That's a wrap on *Danny Boy*! I appreciate everyone's hard work, but I'd especially like to thank my leading lady." Annika looks at Roger, surprised. "Sorry I had to ride you so hard on this one, Annie, but it really paid off. You brought something special to the role. I think it's your best work yet." He takes a glass of champagne from the trays the production staff are passing around and raises his glass. "To Annika!"

"To Annika!" The cry echoes throughout the set and my mother beams graciously at her adoring public.

Soon she joins me carrying two glasses of champagne. "Special occasions call for champagne no matter how young you are." I take a sip and wrinkle my nose. I always thought champagne would be sweeter. Just one of the many disappointments of growing up, I guess.

Clinking her glass against mine, Annika says, "Congratulations, darling, I knew you could do it."

"Thanks, Mom, you were great too. What's your next role?"

"If an interesting indie comes along, I may consider it, but I plan to focus more on old roles for a while." She is smiling in an odd sort of way and I can't help but think she's referring to me. Before it gets totally awkward, a crowd of crew members sweeps her away.

"Nice work today, kid," Roger says. "You were really in the moment."

"It was weird," I tell him. "It felt like I'd *become* Sinead, but I don't know how it happened."

"You could relate to how she'd be feeling and tapped into your own emotions for the performance. But you'll probably find that acting becomes more difficult when you take roles that are different from your real life."

Since he's mellowing with the champagne, I dare to ask, "How can I tap into emotions that I've never felt?"

"Start by studying other people to see how they deal with situations. Use your imagination. Life experience will help, but in the meantime, take classes and learn from your mother."

"I will. Thanks for giving me a chance, Roger."

"You can thank me by being in another one of my films down the road."

"Sure, have your agent call my agent. And by the way, you won't find me listed as the Kid—or Viola, Velma, or even Verna. My name is Vivien Leigh Reid."

Roger laughs. "Okay, I promise I'll get it right in the credits, Veronica."

When he's laughing, he really doesn't look like a troll at all.

★　★　★

Ruby Tooth recognizes me right away. "I told you, kid, no parent, no tattoo. Out with you!"

Sweeping into Celestial Ring in black knee-high boots and a skirt to match, Annika says, "I'd appreciate it if you didn't speak to my daughter in that tone."

Normally, I cringe when she does the whole leather-and-shades movie star entrance, but when Ruby Tooth's face crumples like rotten fruit, I feel an unexpected surge of pride.

"Yes, ma'am," Ruby says. "How may I help you?"

"My daughter and I have just finished shooting a movie and want to get tattoos to commemorate the experience."

Ruby fumbles under the counter for her design catalog. "Of course, ma'am."

"You may call me Ms. Anderson. Now, I'd like to see your certification and some references. I've heard that you're talented, but I can't take any chances: my body is my living, you understand."

I describe the shamrock and heart I saw at Life Art and Ruby immediately flips to the right page. It's even more adorable than I remembered. "Let's get it, Mom."

"All right, darling, if you're certain." To Ruby, she adds, "We would like this on our lower backs. But first I want your assurance that this clover will not turn into a droopy bunch of broccoli in my declining years."

Ruby, who looks ordinary beside my mother despite her colorful body art, says, "The back is the perfect place for it, Ms. Anderson. It will keep its definition."

Mom announces that she will go first, which surprises me. I assumed she'd want to see how mine turned out before mutilating her own body. Instead, she says, "If you don't like it on me, Vivien, you may back out, no questions asked." I have to admit, I'm impressed with her attitude. How many mothers offer to get the first tattoo? Maybe she likes the thought of living dangerously. "I've already booked myself an appointment for a laser treatment in L.A. in case it's a disaster." Or maybe not.

As we follow Ruby Tooth into the back room, Annika babbles nervously the whole time about safety precautions. Finally, she pulls up her blouse. "Watch my back—literally," she whispers to me. "I don't trust her."

"Don't piss her off, Mom. She's the one with the needles."

"Vivien, what did I tell you about using vulgar expressions?"

Seconds later, she teaches me a host of new vulgarities as Ruby Tooth gets down to business.

"It's worse than f—— childbirth," she says through clenched teeth. "At least they gave me an epidural for that." A single tear trickles out from under her sunglasses and down her cheek.

Ruby smiles, the stone in her tooth shining like a tiny drop of blood.

I don't back out. If Mom can take it, so can I.

```
Abs,
I 4giv U 4 ratting me out
2 my parNts.
cuz of U, I hav a Tat2!!!!
My dad iz goin 2 flip.
I hav so much more 2 teL U,
cnt W8 til U cum 2 Seattle!
Leigh
p.s. Maybe U cn visit us in Hollywood
NXT summer 2.
```

★ ★ ★

Finian is quite a sight in his party caftan of shimmering gold. He is demonstrating the Time Warp to Lord Tracy, who's wearing the same battered suit he wore when I first met him, only now he's got a hot pink tie covered in tiny blow-dryers, brushes, and lipsticks.

Thanks to Mom, I'm holding my own in the glamour department with my new boots, low-slung miniskirt, and camisole top. Mrs. O keeps yanking the skirt up onto my waist. I don't bother to fight; all it will get me is a shower of cigarette ash. However, I do point out that my mother, in her sequined halter top and skirt, is showing far more skin than I am as she swans around the club.

At least Annika has had enough champagne to be charming to Rory. Yes, that's Rory of Terminal Burger fame. Yesterday, Colleen and I tracked him down in the frozen food aisle of Dunnes grocery store and acted all surprised to see him. After picking up a bag of frozen peas as a prop, Colleen laid the groundwork by telling him all about *Danny Boy*. Then she stared at me until I finally blurted out an invitation to the wrap party. "I thought my bloody hand would perish from the cold," she said later.

Saying good-bye to her tonight isn't easy. Colleen and Fin have been such good friends to me this summer that I am glum over the thought of leaving them.

"We'll stay in touch," Colleen says, patting my arm. "That's what e-mail is for."

"But it won't be the same as seeing you every day. What's the point of making new friends if it's only for six weeks?"

"We'll meet again down the road. You'd be surprised how often paths cross in the film business. But even if they don't, any friendship is worthwhile, no matter how brief. I learn something from every one."

"Yeah? What did you learn from me?"

"I learned I never want to be a teenager again!" Colleen laughs, but she hugs me and adds, "You reminded me about how important it is to take risks."

"I did? Cool!" I'm proud, but confused. "How?"

"You really pushed yourself this summer, both with acting and with your mother. I was impressed."

Finian comes over and joins our group hug. "Mission accomplished, Colleen," he says. "Now we have someplace to stay in Seattle."

"You're welcome to sleep on my bedroom floor anytime," I say, imagining my father's expression at the sight of the gold cord woven through Fin's braid.

Mom soon drags Colleen and Fin off to the bar, leaving me alone with Rory, who is looking "bleedin' lovely," as Colleen would say, in his baggy jeans and untucked purple shirt. I'd say he's the best-looking guy in the room, except that Sean is here too. Ireland's damp climate sure breeds gorgeous men. I can't for the life of me remember why I got so bent out of shape over Glen Myers.

"Your mom's pretty cool," Rory says, offering me his soda.

"She's all right," I say, accepting his drink. I could get my own, of course, but I'd rather share his. It shows we're a couple.

"And beautiful, too." I'm about to hand his soda back in disgust when he adds, "You look a lot like her."

Rory is actually blushing. He must mean it. I pause for a moment to focus on my breathing, just like Fin taught me. Then I smile and thank him for the compliment. No argument, no denial, no pointing out the beetle on my cheek. Tonight I actually feel as pretty as Mom.

Sean, who has obviously had a few pints, slumps into a chair beside Rory. "What's your IQ, kid?" he demands.

Rory shakes his head. "I don't know."

"Well, you'd better find out—your girlfriend is obsessed. Never stops talking about how smart she is."

"*Sean!*" I could not be more mortified.

"And I don't know about those piercings, pal. They'll limit the roles you get."

Rory looks baffled. "But I don't want to act."

"Oh?" says Sean, raising one eyebrow at me. "But what else is there?"

"I'm thinking of medicine."

"Ya wanker."

"*Sean!*"

What did I ever see in this guy? But when Sean walks away, Rory asks if I could get his autograph—for his mother, he says. In Ireland, Sean Finlay already has quite a following and not just with girls.

I tow Rory across the room to where Finian stands wringing his hands and moaning, "No, Baby Doll, no." My mother is flaunting her tattoo again. I haven't shown mine to anyone, although Colleen spotted it immediately. I think Rory noticed it too, but is too much of a gentleman to say so, since it would mean he was checking out my butt.

My mother insists on introducing me to a reporter from *Bray People* and by the time he has taken our photo, Fin has dragged Rory onto the dance floor along with Mary and Maude. I worry that Rory might feel uncomfortable with so many strangers, but he waves at me to prove that he's having a blast.

Annika looks over at Rory and says, "That boy is such a hottie."

I look at her quickly to see if she's joking, but she's not smiling. "That's *Rory*, Mother."

"Did I already meet him? Surely I'd remember how he defiled that lovely face with piercing." She whispers, "Do you think I stand a chance with him?"

My champagne mood goes flat with a hiss. "You can't be serious."

She bursts out laughing and throws her arm around me. "Only about *acting*, darling. Lighten up!"

"Make your next film a comedy, you're hilarious," I say, mimicking her words from the train. "And watch your back. Once I've studied the Reality Method, you're in big trouble."

"Does that mean you've decided to come to L.A. next summer?"

Roger saves me from committing outright. As the song ends, he stands on a chair to assemble the group for a photograph. Finian pushes Rory in beside me. Sean wedges himself in between my mother and me on the other side. We all wrap our arms around each other and smile.

FLASH!

Leigh,
d Foto arrived DIS morn.
who's d lady stNdN
beside yor mom? It L%kz lik
she's warin a bathrobe.
iz Roger d troll n d frnt row?
3 dAz 'til I cum 2 visit Seattle.
U cn fiL me n on evrtng thN.
cnt W8 2 hear yor Irish accent!
Abs

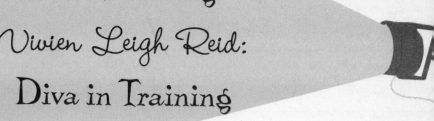

Now Starring
Vivien Leigh Reid:
Diva in Training

Don't miss another outrageously hilarious Vivien Leigh adventure. Stay tuned as Leigh discovers her inner diva when she spends one exciting summer in L.A.

I am trapped in a moving vehicle with a madwoman—a madwoman who claims to be my mother although it's never been proven through genetic testing. We are tearing up the 405 at breakneck speed. Laughing, she maneuvers the Beetle around a lumbering Hummer and cuts off a silver Porsche.

"Are you crazy?" I squawk, as the guy in the Porsche flips her the bird.

"Oh, chill," she says, either to Porsche Guy or me. She yanks down her visor, admires herself in the tiny mirror, and reapplies her lipstick with a flourish.

"Darling, you're so uptight." This time I know she's speaking to me. What's more, I know she is silently adding "just like your father." It's only silent because this is Hour One of my visit to Los Angeles and we have to last six full weeks in the ring.

—from *Now Starring Vivien Leigh Reid: Diva in Training*

A Trade Paperback Original from
🦁 St. Martin's Griffin

Available wherever books are sold Winter 2006